Mary Elizabeth Braddon

Weavers and weft and other tales

Mary Elizabeth Braddon

Weavers and weft and other tales

ISBN/EAN: 9783337137328

Printed in Europe, USA, Canada, Australia, Japan

Cover: Foto ©Andreas Hilbeck / pixelio.de

More available books at **www.hansebooks.com**

WEAVERS AND WEFT

And other Tales

BY THE AUTHOR OF

'LADY AUDLEY'S SECRET'

ETC. ETC. ETC.

IN THREE VOLUMES

VOL. I.

LONDON
JOHN MAXWELL AND CO.
4, SHOE LANE, FLEET STREET
1877

CONTENTS TO VOL. I.

———— ✦ ————

WEAVERS AND WEFT.

CHAPTER I.

AT THE 'STAR AND GARTER.'

GLORIOUS June weather, tender moonlight, from a moon newly risen; silvery on far-off glimpses of the winding river; soft and mysterious where it falls upon the growing darkness of the woodland; a pensive light, by which men, not altogether given up to the world, are apt to ponder the deeper enigmas of this life, and to look backward, Heaven knows with what keen agonies of regret, to youth that has vanished, and friends that are dead.

Two men, who have been dining at the 'Star and Garter,' and who have stolen away from the dessert to

smoke their cigars under the midsummer moon, contemplate the familiar landscape in a lazy meditative
silence.   One is sitting on the stone balustrade of the
terrace, with his face turned to the distant curve of
the river, watching the tender light with a sombre
expression of countenance; the other stands with his
elbows resting on the balustrade, smoking indus-
triously, and looking every now and then with rather
an uneasy glance at his companion.

The first is Sir Cyprian Davenant, the last scion
of a good old Kentish family, and owner of one of
the finest and oldest places in the county of Kent.
The Davenants have been a wild and reckless set for
the last hundred years, and there is not an acre of
Davenant Park or a tree in Davenant woods unen-
cumbered by mortgage.   How Sir Cyprian lives and
contrives to keep out of debt is a subject for the
wonder of his numerous acquaintances.   His intimate friends know that the man has few expensive
habits, and that he has a small income from an estate
inherited from his mother.

Sir Cyprian's companion is a man approaching
middle age, with a decidedly plain face, redeemed

from ugliness by a certain vivacity of expression about the mouth and eyes. This gentleman is James Morton Wyatt, a solicitor, with an excellent practice, and a decided taste for literature and art, which he is rich enough to be able to cultivate at his leisure, leaving the ordinary run of cases to the care of his junior partner, and only putting in an appearance at his office when an affair of some importance is on hand. James Wyatt is a bachelor, and a great favourite with the fair sex, for whom his fashionable modern cynicism seems to possess an extraordinary charm. The cynic has a natural genius for the art of flattery, and a certain subtle power of pleasing that surprises his male acquaintance, who wonder what the women can see in this fellow, with his long, mean-looking nose, small gray eyes, and incessant flow of shallow talk.

'You're not very lively company to-night, Davenant,' James Wyatt said at last. 'I've been waiting with exemplary patience for some kind of reply to the question I asked you about a quarter of an hour ago.'

'You can scarcely expect much liveliness from a

man who is going to start for Africa in four-and-twenty hours, with a very vague prospect of coming back again.'

'Well, I don't know about that. It's a pleasure trip, isn't it, this African exploration business ? '

'It is to be called pleasure, I believe. My share in it would never have come about but for a promise to an old friend. It is a point of honour with me to go. The promise was given five or six years ago, when I was hot upon the subject. I expect very little enjoyment from the business now, but I am bound to go.'

He sighed as he said this, still looking far away at the winding river, with the same gloomy expression in his eyes. It was a face not easily forgotten by those who had once looked upon it, a face of remarkable beauty, a little wan and faded by the cares and dissipations of a career that had been far from perfect. Cyprian Davenant was not quite five-and-thirty, but he had lived at a high pressure rate for ten years of his life, and bore the traces of the fray. The perfect profile, the broad low brow, and deep dark eyes had not lost much in losing the freshness of youth, but the pale cheeks were just a little sunken, and there were lines about those thoughtful eyes, and a weary look about the resolute lips. If there was a fault to be found in the face, it was perhaps the too prominent lower brow, in which the perceptive organs were developed in an extreme degree; yet this very prominence gave character and individuality to the countenance.

James Wyatt heard the regretful sigh, and noted the despondence of his companion's tone.

'I should have thought there were not many people in England you would care about leaving, Davenant,' he said, with a curiously watchful look at the other man's half-averted face, 'I've heard you boast of standing alone in the world.'

'Rather a barren boast, isn't it?' said Sir Cyprian, with a brief and bitter laugh. 'Yes, I am quite alone. Since my sister Marian's marriage, and complete absorption in nursery cares and nursery joys, there is no one to offer let or hindrance to my going yonder. I have friends, of

course, a great many—such as you, Jim, for
instance; jolly good fellows who would smoke
a cigar with me to-night in the bonds of friendship, and who would hear of my death a month
hence without turning a hair.'

'Don't talk platitudes about your friends,
Cyprian. I have no doubt they are as good as
other people's. I don't know a man going more
popular than you are.'

Cyprian Davenant took no notice of this
remark.

'Dear old river,' he murmured tenderly. 'Poor
old river, how many of the happiest hours of my
life have been spent upon your banks, or on your
breast! Shall I ever see you again, I wonder, or
shall I find a grave in some reedy marsh far
away from the Thames and Medway? Don't think
me a sentimental old fool, Jim; but the fact is,
I am a little out of spirits to-night. I ought not
to have accepted Sinclair's invitation. I talked
nineteen to the dozen at dinner, and drank no
end of hock and seltzer, but I felt as dreary as a
ghost assisting at his own funeral. I suppose I

am too old for this African business. I have
outlived the explorer's spirit, and have a foolish
kind of presentiment that the thing will come to
a bad end. Of course I wouldn't own to such a
feeling amongst the men who are going, but I
may confess as much to you without being put
down as a craven.'

'I'll tell you what it is, Davenant,' answered
the lawyer. 'There is something deeper than you
have owned to yet at the bottom of your reluc-
tance to leave England. There is some one, a
least—a woman.'

The other turned his face full upon the speaker.
'You're about right, Jim,' he said, tossing the
end of his cigar away as he spoke. 'There is a
woman, not a sudden caprice either, but a woman
I have loved truly and fondly for the last five
years of my life. If I were a wise man I should
be very glad of this chance of curing my infatuation by putting a few thousand miles between
myself and the loveliest face I ever saw.'

'It's a hopeless case then, I suppose?' suggested
James Wyatt.

'Quite hopeless. What have I to offer the woman I love? The income upon which I have managed to live, since my ruin and subsequent reformation, would be something worse than beggary for a wife such as the woman I love. Even if she were willing to share my poverty, could I be mean enough to drag her into such a slough of despond? No, Jim, it is a hopeless case. My pretty one and I must part,—I to dreary old bachelorhood, she to fulfil her mission, and make one of the grand matches of the season.'

'I think I know the lady,' said James Wyatt, slowly. 'Lord Clanyarde's youngest daughter, the new one, eh, Cyprian? The Clanyardes are neighbours of yours in Kent, I know.'

'Of course I can trust you, Jim. Yes, you've hit it. But what made you fix upon Constance Clanyarde?'

'Have not I senses to understand, and eyes to see? and have I not seen you and Miss Clanyarde together at least three times? Why, Cyprian, the infatuation on both sides is patent to the most unsophisticated observer. It's a pity you've only four hundred a year. That would be rather a tight squeeze for a Clanyarde. They're a notoriously extravagant set, I know, and have been up to their eyes in debt for the last forty years. Yes, I have seen the lady, Cyprian, and she is very lovely. Upon my word I'm sorry for you.'

'Thanks, old fellow. I needn't ask you not to mention my name in conjunction with Miss Clanyarde's. And now I suppose we'd better go back to our friends.'

'I think so. By the way, what do you think of the lady we were asked to meet?'

'Mrs. Walsingham. She is very handsome. A widow, I suppose?'

'She is rather silent on that point, and I have heard it hinted that Colonel Walsingham—he was colonel in the Spanish contingent, I believe, and count of the Holy Roman Empire—still walks this earth, and that the lady owes her agreeable freedom to an American court of divorce. The antecedents are altogether doubtful, and Mrs. Walsingham's society is of the Bohemian order—actors and artists, and nice little women who keep miniature broughams, and don't seem to belong to anybody. Gilbert Sinclair likes that kind of thing.'

'And I suppose Mrs. Walsingham likes Gilbert Sinclair ?'

'Or his money. Sinclair's about the biggest fish in the matrimonial waters, and she will be a happy angler who lands him. But I really believe Mrs. Walsingham has a weakness for the man himself, independent of his money. Strange, isn't it? Sinclair's the dearest fellow in the world, and as his friend, of course, I doat upon him; but I confess that if I were a woman I should regard him with unmitigated loathing.'

'That's rather strong.'

'Of course he's a most estimable creature—out-spoken, frank, liberal, all the manly virtues; but such an unspeakable snob, such a pompous, purse-proud cad. Ah, there he is at the window, looking for us. If I were a woman, you know, Cyprian, that man would be the object of my aversion; but I'm not, and he's my client, and it is the first duty of a solicitor to love his clients. Coming, Gilbert.'

The two men crossed a little bit of lawn, and went in through the open window. The room was lighted with wax candles, and a merry party was crowded round a table, at one end of which a lady was dispensing tea in quite a homelike fashion. She was a very beautiful woman, of a showy type, dressed in India muslin and lace, dressed just a shade too youthfully for her five-and-thirty years. There were two other ladies present, one a fashionable actress, the other her friend and confidante, also an aspirant to dramatic fame. The first was occupied in an agreeable flirtation with a cornet of dragoons; the second was listening with delight to the lively conversation of Mr. Bellingham, the manager of the Phœnix Theatre. A couple of gentlemen belonging to the stockbroking fraternity, and Gilbert Sinclair, the giver of the feast, made up the party.

Mr. Bellingham had been entertaining the company with anecdotes of MacStinger, the great tragedian, the point of every story turning on the discomfiture of the great man by some blundering tyro in dramatic art. Mrs. Walsingham had heard most of the stories a good many times before, and she gave a palpable little yawn as Mr. Bellingham told her how the provincial Horatio informed the great Hamlet that his father's ghost 'would have much *amused* you.' She covered the yawn with her pretty plump little hand, and watched Gilbert Sinclair's face with rather a troubled expression in her own, and in so doing was a little inattentive to the demand for more cups of tea.

Mr. Sinclair was a man whom many people admired, and who was in no obvious manner deserving James Wyatt's unflattering description. He affected a certain bluntness of style, which his friends accepted as evidence of a candid and open soul and a warm heart. He was generous to a lavish degree towards those he associated with and was supposed to like ; but he was not liberal with protestations of regard, and he had few intimate acquaintances. He was a man whom some people called handsome—a big man upwards of six feet high, and with a ponderous, powerful frame. He had large regular features, a florid complexion, prominent reddish brown eyes, thick curling hair, of the same reddish brown, and intensely white teeth.

The chief claim which Mr. Sinclair possessed to
notoriety was comprised in the fact of his wealth.
He was the owner of a great estate in the north,
an estate consisting of ironworks and coalpits, the
annual income from which was said to be something
stupendous, and he had shares in more railways and
mines and foreign loans than his friends could
calculate. His father had been dead about five years,
leaving Gilbert sole possessor of this great fortune,
unfettered by a claim, for the young man was an
only child, and had neither kith nor kin to share
his wealth. He had been at Rugby and Cambridge,
and had travelled all over Europe with a private
tutor. He had seen everything and had been
taught everything that a wealthy young Englishman ought to see or to learn, and had profited in a
very moderate degree by the process. He had a
strong will and a great capacity for keeping his own
secrets, and had started in life with the determination to enjoy existence after his own fashion.
After three years spent in his companionship,
his tutor remarked that he scarcely knew Gilbert
Sinclair any better at the close of their acquaint-

ance than he had known him at the beginning of it.

'And yet the fellow seems so candid,' said Mr. Ashton, the tutor, wonderingly.

'I wish you would give me a little assistance with the teacups, Gilbert,' Mrs. Walsingham said, rather impatiently. 'It is all very well to talk of the pleasantness of having the tea made in the room in this way, but one requires some help. Thanks. Take that to Sir Cyprian Davenant, if you please, and bring me Sophy Morton's cup.'

Mr. Sinclair obeyed, and when he came back with the empty cup Mrs. Walsingham motioned him to a vacant chair by her side, and detained him there till the carriages were announced. She called him by his Christian name in the face of society, and this party of to-night was only one of many entertainments that had been given at different times for her gratification. It was scarcely strange, therefore, if rumour, especially loud on the part of the lady's friends, declared that Mr. Sinclair and Mrs. Walsingham were engaged to be married. But the acquaintance between them had continued for a long

time, and those who knew most of Gilbert Sinclair
shook their heads significantly when the matrimonial question was mooted.

'Gilbert knows his own value,' growled old
Colonel Mordant, an inveterate whist-player and
diner-out, who had introduced young Sinclair into
fast society. 'When he marries he will marry
well. A man with my friend Sinclair's fortune
must have all the advantages in the lady of his
choice—youth, beauty, rank—or, at any rate, position. Most men of that calibre look out for a
corresponding amount of wealth. I don't say
Sinclair will do that. He is rich enough to
indulge in a caprice. But as to marrying Clara
Walsingham—a deuced fine woman, I grant you!
Pas si bête!'

Mrs. Walsingham detained Mr. Sinclair in
conversation some time after the carriages had been
announced. She was very bright and animated,
and looked her best as she talked to him. It was
nearly eleven o'clock when she was reminded of
the lateness of the hour, and the length of the
drive before them, by Miss Sophy Morton, who

had latterly transferred her attention from the callow cornet to Mr. Wyatt, much to the disgust of the youthful dragoon.

'Yes, Sophy, I am just going to put on my shawl. Will you fetch our wraps from the next room, please, Mr. Wyatt? Will you take the back seat in the brougham, Gilbert, and wind up with a lobster salad in Half-moon Street? It is really early, you know.'

'Thanks, no. I could scarcely trust my man to drive those chestnuts, so I think I'll go back in the phaeton; and I'm due at a hop in Eaton Square.'

'Indeed?' asked the lady, curiously, and with a rather anxious look. 'You used not to care for dancing parties.'

'I don't care for them now, but one has to sacrifice inclination now and then, you know.'

'Do I know the people?' asked Mrs. Walsingham.

Mr. Sinclair smiled as he replied, 'I think not.'

A cloud came over the lady's face, and when

her shawl had been adjusted she took Gilbert Sinclair's arm in silence. Nor did she speak to him on the way to the porch of the hotel, where a mail phaeton and a couple of broughams were waiting. Her adieux to the rest of the party were brief and cold, and Gilbert himself she only honoured by a stately inclination of her beautiful head, with its coronal of bright chestnut hair, and coquettish little curls dotted about a broad white forehead.

Mr. Sinclair stood bareheaded under the porch as the Walsingham brougham drove away, and then turned with a frown to perform his duties in other directions. Here, however, he found there was nothing left for him to do. Miss Morton and her companion had been escorted to their carriage by Sir Cyprian Davenant and Mr. Wyatt, and were waiting to bid their host good-bye.

'And a thousand thanks for our delightful day, Mr. Sinclair, which we are not likely to forget for a long time, are we, Imogen?'

Miss Imogen Harlow, who had been born Watson and christened Mary Anne, shook her empty little head coquettishly, and declared that the memory of that Richmond dinner would remain with her to her dying day. And on the way home the two ladies discussed Mr. Sinclair and the probable amount of his income, and speculated as to the chances of his ultimately marrying Mrs. Walsingham.

CHAPTER II.

'WHEN WE TWO PARTED.'

SIR CYPRIAN DAVENANT and James Wyatt went
back to town by rail, and parted company at
Waterloo, the baronet going westward to his
bachelor lodgings in one of the shabbier streets
about Grosvenor Square, the lawyer to a big dull
house in Bloomsbury Square, which his father had
bought and furnished some fifty years before, and
in which there was a large collection of old pictures, and a still larger collection of rare old wines
stored away in great gloomy cellars with ponderous
iron-plated doors. Mr. Wyatt the elder had done a
good deal of business, of a very profitable kind,
with the youthful members of the British
aristocracy, had raised loans for them, at heavy
rates of interest, never omitting to remind them of
the sacrifice they made in borrowing money at all,
and only yielding to the stern necessities of their

position in a reluctant grudging spirit at the last, whereby the foolish young men were in no manner prevented from rushing blindfold along the broad road to ruin, but were kept in ignorance of the fact that it was from Thomas Wyatt's own coffers that the money came, and that to him the interest accrued.

James Wyatt inherited his father's astute mind, together with his father's handsome fortune, and he had cultivated very much the same kind of business, making himself eminently useful to his young friends, and winning for himself the character of a most prudent friend and adviser. He did not take the risks of an ordinary money-lender, and he raised money for his clients on terms that seemed moderate when compared with the usurer's exorbitant demands; but he contrived nevertheless to profit considerably by every transaction, and he never let a client escape him while there was a feather to pluck.

Sir Cyprian Davenant had been in this gentleman's hands ever since his coming of age, but now that there was not an acre of the Davenant estate unmortgaged, and the day was not far off in which must come foreclosure or sale, the relations between the two men were rather those of friendship than business. Cyprian had lived his life, had wasted his last available shilling, and had reformed. His dissipations had never been of a base or degrading order. He had been wild and reckless, had played high at his club, and lost money on the turf, and kept an extravagant stud, and ridden in steeple-chases at home and abroad, and had indulged in many other follies peculiar to his age and station; but he had no low vices, and when his money was gone, and the freshness of youth with it, he fell from the ranks of his fast friends without a sigh. It was too late for him to think of a profession; and there seemed to be no brighter fate possible for him than the dreary monotony of old bachelorhood on a limited income.

'I suppose I shall live to be an old fogy,' he said to himself. 'I shall have my particular corner at the club, and be greedy about the newspapers, and bore the youngsters with my vapid old stories. What a barren waste of years to look forward to!'

Sir Cyprian had work to do after the Richmond

dinner, and was occupied till long after daybreak
with letter-writing, and the last details of his pack-
ing.   When all was done he was still wakeful, and
sat by his writing-table in the morning sunlight,
thinking of the past and the future with a gloomy
face.

Thinking of the past—of all those careless hours
in which one bright girlish face had been the chief
influence of his life ; thinking of the future, in which
he was to see that sweet face no more.

'How happy we have been together!' he thought,
as he bent over a photograph framed in the lid of his
despatch-box, contemplating the lovely face with a
fond smile, and a tender dreaming look in his dark
eyes.   'What long hours of boredom I have gone
through in the way of evening parties in order to
get a waltz with her, or a few minutes of quiet
talk in some balcony or conservatory, and all for the
vain delight of loving her! Without one ray of hope
for the future, with the knowledge that I was doing
her a great wrong in following her up so closely with
my barren love.   So even James Wyatt saw my
infatuation! And hers, he said. Is there any truth

in that last assertion, I wonder? Does Constance really care for me? I have never asked her the question, never betrayed myself by any direct avowal. Yet these things make themselves understood somehow, and I think my darling knows that I would willingly die for her: and I think I know that she will never care for any man as she could care for me!'

He shut the despatch-box, and began to walk slowly up and down the room, thinking.

'There would be just time for me to do it,' he said to himself presently; 'just time for me to run down to Davenant, and see the old place once more. It will be sold before I come back from Africa, if ever I do come back. And there would be the chance of seeing her. I know the Clanyardes have gone back to Kent. Yes, I will run down to Davenant for a few hours. A man must be hard indeed who does not care to give one farewell look at the house in which the brightest years of his life have been spent. And I may see her again, only to say good-bye, and to see if she is sorry for my going. What more can I say to her? What more need be

said? She knows that I would lay down my life
for her.'

He went to his room, and slept a kind of fitful
sleep until eight o'clock, when he woke with a start,
and began to dress for his journey. At nine he was
driving through the streets in a hansom, and at mid-
day he was in one of the woody lanes leading across
country from the little Kentish railway station to his
own ancestral domain, the place he had once been
proud and fond of, but which he looked at now in
bitterness of spirit, and with a passionate regret. The
estate had been much encumbered when it fell into
his hands, but he knew that, with prudence, he might
have saved the greater part of it.

He entered the park by a rustic gateway, beside
which there was a keeper's lodge, a gate dividing the
thickest part of the wood from a broad green valley,
where the fern grew deep under the spreading
branches of giant oaks, and around the smooth silvery trunks of fine old beeches. The Davenant
timber had suffered little from the prodigal's de-
stroying hand. He could better endure the loss of
the place than its desecration.

The woman at the keeper's lodge welcomed her master with an exclamation of surprise.

'I hope you have come to stay, Sir Cyprian,' she said, dropping a rustic curtsey.

'No, Mrs. Mead, I have only come for a last look at the old place before I go away from England.'

'Going away, sir! that's bad news.'

Cyprian cut short her lamentations with a friendly nod, and was walking on, when it suddenly struck him that the woman might be useful.

'Oh, by the way,' he said, 'Lord Clanyarde is at Marchbrook, is he not?'

'Yes, sir, the family have been there for the last week.'

'Then I'll walk over there before I go on to the house, if you'll unlock the gate again, Mrs. Mead.'

'Shall I send one of my boys to the house with a message, sir, about dinner, or anything?'

'You are very good. Yes, you can send the lad to tell old Mrs. Pomfret to get me something to eat at six o'clock, if you please. I must get back to London by the 7.30 train.'

'Deary me, sir, going back so soon as that?'

The gates of Marchbrook were about half a mile distant from the keeper's lodge. Lord Clanyarde's house was a dreary red brick habitation, of the Georgian era, with long lines of narrow windows looking out upon a blank expanse of pasture land, by courtesy a park. An avenue of elms led from the lodge gate to the southern front of the house, and on the western side there was a prim Dutch garden, divided from the park by a ha-ha. The place was in perfect order, but there was a cold, bare look about everything that was eminently suggestive of narrow means.

A woman at the lodge informed Sir Cyprian that there was no one at home. Lord Clanyarde had driven to Maidstone. Miss Clanyarde was in the village; she had gone to see the children at the National School. She would be home at two, to lunch, no doubt, according to her usual habit. She was very fond of the school, and sometimes spent her morning in teaching the children.

'But they leave school at twelve, don't they?' demanded Sir Cyprian.

'Yes, sir; but I dare say Miss Constance has

stopped to talk to Miss Evans, the schoolmistress. She is a very genteel young person, and quite a favourite with our ladies.'

Cyprian Davenant knew the little school-house, and the road by which Constance Clanyarde must return from her mission. Nothing could be more pleasant to him than the idea of meeting her in her solitary walk. He turned away from the lodge-keeper, muttering something vague about calling again later, and walked at a rapid pace to the neighbouring village, which consisted of two straggling rows of old-fashioned cottages fringing the skirts of a common. Close to the old ivy-covered church, with its massive square tower and grass-grown grave-yard, there was a modern Gothic building in which the village children struggled through the difficulties of an educational course, and from the open windows whereof their youthful voices rang loudly out upon the summer air every morning in a choral version of the multiplication table.

Miss Clanyarde was standing in the little stone porch talking to the schoolmistress when Sir Cyprian opened the low wooden gate. She looked

up at the sound of his footstep with a sudden
blush.

'I did not know you were at Davenant, Sir
Cyprian,' he said, with some little embarrassment,
as they shook hands.

'I have not been at Davenant, Miss Clanyarde.
I only left town this morning. I have come down
here to say good-bye to Davenant and all old
friends.'

The blush faded, and left the lovely face very
pale.

'Is it true that you are going to Africa? I heard
from some friends in town that you were to join
Captain Harcourt's expedition.'

'It is quite true. I promised Harcourt some
years ago that if he ever went again I would go with
him.'

'And you are pleased to go, I suppose?'

'No, Miss Clanyarde, not pleased to go. But I
think that sort of thing is about the best employ-
ment for the energies of a waif and stray, such as I
am. I have lived my life, you see, and have not a
single card left to play in the game of civilized

existence.   There is some hope of adventure out yonder.   Are you going home?'

'Yes, I was just saying good-bye to Miss Evans as you came in.'

'Then I'll walk back to Marchbrook with you, if you'll allow me.   I told the lodge-keeper I would return by and by in the hope of seeing Lord Clanyarde.'

'You have been to Marchbrook already, then?'

'Yes, and they told me at the lodge that I should find you here.'

After this there came rather an awkward silence. They walked away from the school-house side by side, Sir Cyprian furtively watchful of his companion's face, in which there were signs of a sorrow that seemed something deeper than the conventional regret which a fashionable beauty might express for the departure of a favourite waltzer.

The silence was not broken until they had arrived at a point where two roads met, the turnpike road to Marchbrook, and a shady lane, a cross country road, above which the overarching branches of the elms made a roof of foliage in this midsummer

season. There was a way of reaching Marchbrook
by this lane, a tempting walk compared to the high
road.

'Let us go back by the lane,' said Cyprian. 'It is
a little longer, but I am sure you are not in a hurry.
You would have dawdled away half the morning
talking to that young woman at the school if I hadn't
come to fetch you, and it will be our last walk
together, Constance. I may call you Constance, may
I not, as I used when you were in the nursery ? I
am entitled to a few dismal privileges, like a dying
man, you know. Oh, Constance, what happy hours
we have spent together in these Kentish lanes ! I
shall see them in my dreams out yonder, and your
face will shine down upon me from a background of
green leaves and blue sky ; and then I shall awake
to find myself camping out upon some stretch of
barren sand, with jackals howling in the distance.'

'What a dreadful picture !' said Constance, with
a faint forced laugh. 'But if you are so reluctant to
leave England, why do you persist in this African
expedition ?'

'It is a point of honour with me to keep my

promise; and it is better for me to be away from England.'

'You are the best judge of that question.'

Sir Cyprian was slow to reply to this remark. He had come down to Kent upon a sudden impulse, determined in no manner to betray his own folly, and bent only upon snatching the vain delight of a farewell interview with the girl he loved. But to be with her, and not to tell her the truth was more difficult than he had imagined. He could see that she was sorry for his departure, he believed that she loved him, but he knew enough of Viscount Clanyarde's principles and his daughter's education to know there would be something worse than cruelty in asking this girl to share his broken fortunes.

'Yes, Constance,' he went on, 'it is better for me to be away. So long as I am here it is the old story of the insect and the flame. I cannot keep out of temptation. I cannot keep myself from haunting the places where I am likely to meet the girl I love, fondly, foolishly, hopelessly. Don't look at me with those astonished eyes, my darling. You must have known my secret ever so long. I meant to keep silence till the end; but you see the words are spoken in spite of me. My love, I dare not ask you to be my wife. I dare only tell you that no other woman will ever bear that name. You are not angry with me, Constance, for having spoken?'

'Angry with you——' she began, and then broke down utterly, and burst into tears.

He drew his arm round her with a tender protecting gesture, and soothed her gently, as if she had been a child.

'Dear love, I am not worth your tears. If I had been a better man I might have redeemed Davenant by this time, and might have hoped to make you my wife. There would have been some hope for me, would there not, dear, if I could have offered you a home that your father could approve?'

'I am not so mercenary as you think me,' answered Constance, drying her tears, and disengaging herself from Sir Cyprian's encircling arm. 'I am not afraid of poverty. But I know that my father would never forgive——'

'And I know it too, my dearest girl, and you shall not be asked to break with your father for such a man as I. I never meant to speak of this, dear, but perhaps it is better that I should have spoken. You will soon forget me, Constance, and I shall hear of you making some brilliant marriage before I have been away very long. God grant the man may be worthy of you. God grant you may marry a good man.'

' I am not very likely to marry,' replied Miss Clanyarde.

' My dearest, it is not possible you can escape. Heaven forbid that my shadow should come between you and a happy future. It is enough for one of us to carry the burden of a life-long regret.'

There was much more talk between them before they arrived at a little gate opening into the March-brook kitchen-garden ; fond regretful talk of the days that were gone, in which they had been so much together down in Kent, with all the freedom permitted between friends and neighbours of long standing, the days before Constance had made her *début* in the great world.

Sir Cyprian did not persevere in his talked-of visit to Lord Clanyarde. He had, in truth, very little

desire to see that gentleman. At the little garden
gate he took Miss Clanyarde's two hands in his own
with one fond fervent clasp.

'You know the old song,' he said, ' "it may be
for years, and it may be for ever." It *is* an eternal
parting for me, darling, for I can never hope to call
you by that sweet name again. You have been
very good to me in letting me speak so freely to-day,
and it is a kind of consolation to have told you my
sorrow. God bless you, and good-bye.'

This was their parting. Sir Cyprian went back
to Davenant, and spent a dreary hour in walking up
and down the corridor, and looking into the empty
rooms. He remembered them tenanted by the loved
and lost. How dismal they were now in their blank
and unoccupied state! and how little likelihood
there was that he should ever see them again! His
dinner was served for him in a pretty breakfast-room,
with a bow-window overlooking a garden that had
been his mother's delight, and where the roses she
had loved still blossomed in all their glory. The
memory of the dead was with him as he eat his
solitary meal, and he was glad when it was time for

him to leave the great desolate house, in which every door closed with a dismal reverberation, as if it had been shutting upon a vault.

He left Davenant immediately after dinner, and walked back to the little station, thinking mournfully enough of his day's work, and of the life that lay before him. Before noon next day he and his companions were on the first stage of their journey, speeding towards Marseilles.

CHAPTER III.

NEARLY a year had gone since Cyprian Davenant turned his back upon British soil. It was the end of May, high season in London, and unusually brilliant weather, the West End streets and squares thronged with carriages, and everywhere throughout that aristocratic western world a delightful flutter and buzz of life and gaiety; as if the children of that pleasant region had indeed in some manner secured an exemption from the cares and sorrows of meaner mortals, and were bent on making the most of their privileged existence.

A neatly appointed brougham waited before the door of a house in Half-moon Street, and had been waiting there for some time. It was Mrs. Walsingham's brougham, and the lady herself was slowly pacing up and down her little drawing-room, pausing every now and then to look out of the window and

in a very unpleasant state of mind. She was dressed
for walking, in one of those airy combinations of
India muslin and fine old lace which she so much
affected, her warm brown hair crowned with a
bonnet that seemed to be made of pansies, and she
was looking very handsome, in spite of the cloud
upon her brow, and a certain angry sparkle in her eyes·

'I suppose he is not coming,' she muttered at
last, tossing her white silk umbrella upon the table
with a petulant gesture. 'This will be the second
disappointment in a week. But I shall not go to
the concert without him. What do I care for their
tiresome classical music, Hummel, and Chopin, and
all the rest of them, or to be stared at by a crowd of
great ladies who don't choose to know me?'

She rang the bell violently, but before it could
be answered there came a thundering double knock
at the door below, and a minute afterwards Gilbert
Sinclair dashed into the room.

'Late again, Gilbert,' cried Mrs. Walsingham,
reproachfully, her face brightening nevertheless at
his coming, and kindling with a pleased welcoming
smile as they shook hands.

'Yes, I know, it's late for that confounded concert. But I want you to let me off that infliction, Clara. That sort of thing is such a consummate bore to a man who doesn't know the difference between Balfe and Beethoven, and you know I have a heap of engagements on my hands.'

'You have only come to cry off, then?' said Mrs. Walsingham, with a sudden contraction of her firmly moulded lips.

'My dear Clara, how demoniac you can look when you like! But I wouldn't cultivate that kind of expression if I were you. Of course I'll go to the concert with you if you are bent upon it, rather than run the risk of anything in the way of a scene. But you know very well that I don't care for music, and you ought to know——'

He stopped, hesitating, with a furtive look in his red-brown eyes, and a nervous action of one big hand about his thick brown moustache.

'I ought to know what, Mr. Sinclair?' asked Clara Walsingham, with a sudden hardness of voice and manner.

'That it is good neither for your reputation nor

mine that we should be seen so often together at such places as this Portman Square concert. It is almost a private affair, you know, and everybody present will know all about us.'

'Indeed! and since when has Mr. Gilbert Sinclair become so careful of his reputation—or of mine?'

'Since you set your friends talking about our being engaged to be married, Mrs. Walsingham. You have rather too many feminine acquaintances with long tongues. I don't like being congratulated —or chaffed—it comes to pretty much the same thing—upon an event which you and I know can never happen.'

'Never is a long word, Gilbert. My husband may die, and leave me free to become your wife; if you should do me the honour to repeat the proposal which you made to me six years ago.'

'I don't like waiting for dead men's shoes, Clara,' answered Sinclair, in rather a sulky tone. 'I made you that offer in all good faith, when I believed you to be a widow, and when I was madly in love with you; but six years is a long time, and——'

He broke down again, and stood before her with his eyes fixed on the ground.

'And men are fickle,' she said, taking up his unfinished sentence. 'What is that Alfred de Musset says?'—

> "C'est l'histoire du cœur.—Tout va si vite en lui!
>
> Tout y meurt, comme un son, tout, excepté l'ennui!"

That is what a man says of himself, you know. The woman in the story is constant—constant in her love and constant in her revenge. You have grown tired of me, Gilbert, is that what you mean?'

'Not exactly that, Clara, but rather tired of a position that keeps me a single man without a single man's liberty. You are quite as exacting as a wife, more jealous than a mistress; and I am getting to an age now at which a man begins to feel a kind of yearning for something more like a home than chambers in the Albany, some one more like a wife than a lady who requires one to be perpetually playing the *cavaliere servente*.'

'Have I been exacting, Gilbert? I did not know that. I have tried my uttermost to make my house agreeable to you. Believe me, I care less for gaiety than you imagine. I should be satisfied with a very dull life if I saw you often. Oh, Gilbert, I think you ought to know how well I love you.'

'I could better have believed that six years ago, if you had consented to leave England with me, as I proposed, when I found out the secret of Colonel Walsingham's existence, and that the Yankee divorce was all bosh.'

'I loved you too well to sink as low as that, Gilbert.'

'I thought the strength of a woman's love was best shown by her sacrifice of self. You preferred your reputation to my happiness, and have kept me dangling on ever since, for the gratification of your vanity, I suppose. It would have been more generous to have dismissed me, and made an end of the farce at once.'

'You were not so willing to be dismissed until very lately, Gilbert. You were quite willing that we should continue friends, with the hope that the future might make us something nearer and dearer. Why have you grown so tired of me all of a sudden?'

'I tell you again, it is the position I am tired of, not you. If you were free to marry me it would be a different thing, of course. As it is we are both wasting our lives, and getting ourselves talked about into the bargain.'

Clara Walsingham laughed scornfully at this.

'I care very little what people say of me,' she said. 'English society has not chosen to receive me very graciously, and I feel myself at liberty to despise its petty by-laws. Nor did I think you would consider yourself injured by having your name linked with mine.'

'But you see, Clara, it does a man harm to have it said he is engaged to a woman he never can marry. It does him some kind of harm in certain circles.'

'How vague you are, Gilbert, and how mysterious! Some kind of harm in certain circles. What does that mean?'

She stood for a minute looking at him, with a sudden intensity in her face. He kept his eyes on the ground during that sharp scrutiny, but he was fully conscious of it nevertheless.

'Gilbert Sinclair,' she cried, after a long pause, 'you are in love with some other woman. You are going to jilt me.'

There was a suppressed agony in her tone which both surprised and alarmed the man to whom she spoke. Of late he had doubted the sincerity of her attachment to him, and had fostered that doubt, telling himself that it was his wealth she cared for.

'Would it grieve you very much if I were to marry, Clara?' he asked.

'Grieve me if you were to marry! It would be the end of my life. I would never forgive you. But you are playing with me. You are only trying to frighten me.'

'You are frightening yourself,' he answered. 'I only put the question in a speculative way. Let us drop the subject. If you want to go to the concert——'

'I don't want to go; I am not fit to go anywhere. Will you ring that bell, please? I shall send the brougham back to the stable.'

'Won't you drive in the park this fine afternoon?'

'No; I am fit for nothing now.'

A maid-servant came in answer to the bell.

'You can take my bonnet, Filby,' said Mrs. Walsingham, removing that floral structure, 'and tell Johnson I shall not want the brougham to-day. You'll stop to dinner, won't you, Gilbert?' she went on when the maid had retired. 'Mr. Wyatt is to be here, and Sophy Morton.'

'How fond you are of those actor people! So Jim Wyatt is coming, is he? I rather want to see him. But I have other engagements this afternoon, and I really don't think I can stay.'.

'Oh, yes, you can, Gilbert. I shall think I had just grounds for my suspicion if you are so eager to run away.'

'Very well, Clara, if you make a point of it I will stop.'

Mr. Sinclair threw himself into one of the low luxurious chairs, with an air of resignation scarcely complimentary to his hostess. Time was when this woman had exercised a profound power over him, when he had been indeed eager to make her his wife; but that time was past and gone. He was tired of an alliance which demanded from him more than it was in his selfish nature to give; and he was inclined to be angry with himself for having wasted so much of his life upon an infatuation which he now accounted the one supreme mistake of his career. Before his charmed eyes there had appeared a vision of womanly loveliness compared with which Clara Walsingham's beauty seemed of the earth, earthy. He could not deny that she was beautiful, but in that other girlish face there was a magic which he had never before encountered, a glamour that enthralled his narrow soul.

The interval before dinner dragged wearily, in spite of Mrs. Walsingham's efforts to sustain a pleasant conversation about trifles. Gilbert was not to be beguiled into animated discussion upon any subject whatever. It seemed as if the two were treading cautiously upon the verge of some conver-sational abyss, some dangerous chasm, into whose depths they might at any moment descend with a sudden plunge.

Mrs. Walsingham questioned her companion about his plans for the end of the season.

'Shall you go to Norway for the salmon fishing?'
she asked.

'I think not. I am tired of that part of the
world.'

'Then I suppose you will amuse yourself with
the grouse in Scotland?'

'No, I have just declined a share in a moor. I
am heartily sick of grouse shooting. I have really
no settled plans as yet. I shall contrive to get rid
of the autumn somehow, no doubt.'

The conversation dawdled on in this languid
manner for a couple of hours, and then Mr. Sinclair
went away to change his loose gray suit for the
regulation evening dress.

The smile which Mrs. Walsingham's face had worn
while she talked to him faded the moment he had
left her, and she began to pace the room with rapid
steps and a clouded brow.

'Yes, there is no doubt of it,' she muttered to
herself, with suppressed passion. 'I have seen the
change in him for the last twelve months. There is
some one else. How should I lose him if it were not
so? Heaven knows what pains I have taken to

retain my hold upon him !   There is some one else.
He is afraid to tell me the truth.   He is wise in that
respect.   Who can the woman be for whom I am to
be forsaken ?   He knows so many people, and visits
so much, and is everywhere courted and flattered on
account of his money.   Oh, Gilbert, fool, fool !
Will any woman ever love you as I have loved you,
for your own sake, without a thought of your fortune, with a blind idolatry which has made me
indifferent to your faults ?   What is it that I love
in him, I wonder?   I know that he is not a good
man.   I have seen his heartlessness too often of
late not to know that he is hard and cruel and
remorseless towards those who come between
him and his iron will.   But I, too, could be hard
and remorseless if a great wrong were done me.
Yes, even to him.   Let him take care how he pro-
vokes a passionate, reckless nature like mine.   Let
him beware of playing with fire.'

This was the gist of her thoughts during a
gloomy reverie that lasted more than an hour.   At
the end of that time Miss Morton was announced,
and came fluttering into the room, resplendent in

rose-coloured silk and black lace, followed shortly
by James Wyatt, the lawyer, courteous and debon-
nair, full of small talk and the latest fashionable
scandal.   Gilbert Sinclair was the last to enter.

The dinner was elegantly served in a pretty little
dining-room, hung with pale green draperies, and
adorned with a few clever water-colour pictures, a
room in which there was a delightful air of cool-
ness and repose.   The folding-doors between the two
rooms on the ground-floor had been removed, and
the back room was covered with a cool Indian
matting, and converted into a kind of conservatory
for large ferns and orange trees, the dark foliage
whereof made an agreeable background to the pollard
oak furniture in the dining-room.   There was no
profuse display of plate upon the round table, but
the wine flasks and tall-stemmed glasses were old
Venetian, and the dessert service was old Wedge-
wood.

Mr. Wyatt was invaluable in the task of sustain-
ing the conversation, and Clara Walsingham seconded
him admirably, though there was a sharp anguish at
her heart that was now almost an habitual pain, an

agony prophetic of a coming blow. Gilbert Sinclair
was a little brighter than he had been in the afternoon, and contributed his share to the talk with a
decent grace, only once or twice betraying absence
of mind by a careless answer and a wandering look
in his big brown eyes.

James Wyatt and Mrs. Walsingham had been
running through a catalogue of the changes of
fortune, for good or evil, that had befallen their
common acquaintances, when Gilbert broke in upon
their talk suddenly with the question,—

'What has become of that fellow who dined with
us at Richmond last year ?   Sir Cyprian something.'

'Sir Cyprian Daveuant,' said James Wyatt. 'He
is still in Africa.'

'In Africa ; ah, yes, to be sure, I remember
hearing that he was going to join Harcourt's expedition. I was not much impressed by him, though I
had heard him talked about as something out of the
common way. He had precious little to say for
himself.'

'You saw him at a disadvantage that day. He
was out of spirits at leaving England.'

'Very likely; but I had met him in society very often before. He's rather a well-looking fellow, no doubt; but I certainly couldn't discover any special merit in him beyond his good looks. He's a near neighbour of the Clanyardes, by the way, when he's at home, is he not?'

'When he's at home, yes,' answered the solicitor. 'But I doubt if ever he'll go home again.'

'You mean that he'll come by his death in Africa, I suppose?'

'I sincerely hope not, for Cyprian Davenant is one of my oldest friends. No, I mean that he's not very likely to see the inside of his ancestral halls any more. The place is to be sold this year.'

'The baronet is quite cleaned out, then?'

'He has about four hundred a year which he inherited from his mother, so tightly tied up that he has not been able to make away with it.'

'What Clanyardes are those?' asked Mrs. Walsingham.

'Viscount Clanyarde and his family. They have a place called Marchbrook, and a very poor place it is, the adjoining estate to Davenant. The old Viscount is as poor as Job.'

'Indeed. But his youngest daughter will make a great match, no doubt, and redeem the fortunes of the house. I saw her at the opera the other night. She was pointed out to me as the loveliest girl in London, and I really think she has a right to be called so. What do you think of her, Gilbert ?'

She fixed her eyes upon Sinclair with a sudden scrutiny that took him off his guard. A dusky flush came over his face, and he hesitated awkwardly before replying to her very simple question.

Clara Walsingham's heart gave a great throb.

'That is the woman,' she said to herself.

'Miss Clanyarde is very handsome,' stammered Gilbert, 'at least, I believe that is the general opinion about her. She has been intimate with your friend Davenant ever since she was a child, hasn't she, Wyatt ?' he asked, with an indifference of tone which one listener knew to be assumed.

'Yes, I have heard him say as much,' the other answered, with an air of reserve which implied the

possession of more knowledge upon this point than
he cared to impart.

'Those acquaintances of the nursery are apt to
end in something more than friendship,' said Mrs.
Walsingham. 'Is there any engagement between
Sir Cyprian and Miss Clanyarde ? '

'Decidedly not.'

Gilbert Sinclair burst into a harsh laugh.

'Not very likely,' he exclaimed. 'I should like
to see old Clanyarde's face if his daughter talked of
marrying a gentlemanly pauper.'

'That is the woman he loves,' Mrs. Walsingham
repeated to herself.

No more was said about Sir Cyprian or the
Clanyardes. The conversation drifted into other
channels, and the evening wore itself away more or
less pleasantly, with the assistance of music by and
by in the drawing-room, where there were a few
agreeable droppers in. Mrs. Walsingham played
brilliantly, and possessed a fine mezzo-soprano, which
had been cultivated to an extreme degree. There
were those who said she had been an opera singer
before her marriage with that notorious *roué* and

reprobate, Vernon Walsingham.   But this was not
true.   Clara Walsingham's musical powers had never
been exercised professionally.   She had a real love
of music, for its own sake, and found consolation
during many desolate hours in the companionship of
her piano.

CHAPTER IV.

THREE days after the little dinner in Half-moon Street, Mrs. Walsingham sat at her solitary breakfast-table rather later than usual, dawdling over the morning papers, and wondering drearily what she should do with the summer day before her. She had seen nothing of Gilbert Sinclair since the dinner, and had endured an agony of self-torment in the interval. His name appeared in one of the morning journals among the guests at a distinguished countess's ball on the previous evening, and in the list of names above Mr. Sinclair's she found those of Lord Clanyarde and his daughter. There had been a time when Gilbert set his face against all fashionable entertainments, voting them the abomination of desolation. He had changed of late, and went everywhere, raising fond hopes in the breasts of anxious mothers with large broods of marriageable daughters, waiting for their promotion.

Mrs. Walsingham sat for some time looking vacantly at the long list of names, and thinking of the man she loved. Yes, she loved him. She knew his character by heart, knew how nearly that obstinate selfish nature verged upon brutality, and loved him nevertheless. Something in the force of his character exercised a charm over her own ill-regulated mind. She had believed in the strength of his affection for herself, which had been shown in a passionate undisciplined kind of manner, that blinded her to the shallowness of the sentiment. She had been intensely proud of her power over this rough Hercules, all the more proud of his subjugation because of that half-hidden brutishness which she had long ago divined in him. She liked him for what he was, and scarcely wished him to be better than he was. She only wanted him to be true to her. When he had asked her, years ago, to be his wife, she had frankly told him the story of her youth and marriage. Her husband was five-and-twenty years her senior, a man with a constitution broken by nearly half a century of hard living, and she looked forward hopefully to a speedy release from a

union that had long been hateful to her. She had
believed that it would be possible to retain Gilbert's
affection until the time when that release should
come without sacrifice of honour or reputation. Had
she not believed and hoped this, it is impossible to say
what guilty sacrifice she might not have been willing
to make rather than lose the man she loved. She
had hoped to keep him dangling on, governed by her
womanly tact, a faithful slave, until the Colonel—who
led a stormy kind of existence, wandering about the
Continent, haunting German gaming-tables, and
plucking English pigeons—should be good enough to
depart this life. But the Colonel was a long time
exhausting his battered constitution, and the flowery
chain in which Mrs. Walsingham held her captive
had faded considerably with the passage of years.

A loud double knock startled the lady from her
reverie. Who could such an early visitor be?
Gilbert himself, perhaps. He had one of those
exceptional constitutions to which fatigue is a
stranger, and would be no later astir to-day because
of last night's ball. Her heart fluttered hopefully,
but sank again with the familiar anguish of dis-

appointment as the door was opened and a low
deferential voice made itself heard in the hall.
Those courteous tones did not belong to Gilbert
Sinclair.

A card was brought to her presently, with James
Wyatt's name upon it, and 'On special business,
with many apologies,' written in pencil below the
name in the solicitor's neat hand.

'Shall I show the gentleman to the drawing-
room, ma'am, or will you see him here?' asked the
servant.

'Ask him to come in here. What special business can Mr. Wyatt have with me?' she wondered.

The solicitor came into the room as she asked
herself this question, looking very fresh and bright in
his careful morning costume. He was more careful
of his toilet than many handsomer men, and knew
how far the elegance of his figure and the perfection
of his dress went to atone for his plain face.

'My dear Mrs. Walsingham,' he began, 'I owe
you a thousand apologies for this unseasonable
intrusion. If I did not think the nature of my business would excuse——'

'There is nothing to be excused. You find me guilty of a very late breakfast, that is all. Why should you not call at half-past ten as well as at half-past three? It is very kind of you to come at all.'

There was a tone of indifference in all this politeness, a half weary tone, which did not fail to strike James Wyatt. He had made this woman a study during the last year, and he knew every note of her voice, every expression of her face.

'I hold it one of my dearest privileges to be received by you,' he replied, with a certain grave tenderness. 'There are some men who do not know when they are happy, Mrs. Walsingham. I am not one of those.'

She looked at him with a surprise that was half scornful.

'Pray spare me the pretty speeches which make you so popular with other women,' she said. 'You spoke of business just now. Did you really mean business?'

'Not in a legal sense. My errand this morning is of rather a delicate nature. I would not for the

world distress or offend you by any unwarranted
allusion to your domestic relations, but I believe I
am the bearer of news which can scarcely have
reached you yet by any other channel, and which
may not be altogether unwelcome.'

'What news can you possibly bring me?' she
asked, with a startled look.

'Would it distress you to hear that Colonel
Walsingham is ill—dangerously ill, even?'

Her breath came quicker as he spoke.

'I am not hypocrite enough to pretend that,' she
answered. 'My heart has long been dead to any
feeling but anger—I will not say hatred, though he
has deserved as much—where that man is concerned. I have suffered too much by my union
with him.'

'Then let me be the first to congratulate you
upon your release from bondage. Your husband is
dead.'

Clara Walsingham's cheek blanched, and she
was silent for some moments; and then she asked in
a steady voice, 'How did you come by the news of
his death?'

'In the simplest and most natural manner. My business requires me to be *au courant* as to Continental affairs, and I get several French and German newspapers. In one of the last I found the account of a duel, succeeding upon a quarrel at the gaming-table, in which your husband fell, shot through the lungs. He only survived a few hours. His opponent was a Frenchman, and is now under arrest. Shall I read you the paragraph?'

'If you please,' answered Mrs. Walsingham, with perfect calmness of manner. Her heart was beating tumultuously nevertheless. She had a dismal conviction that no advantage—that is to say, not that one advantage for which she longed—would come to her from her husband's death. How eagerly she had desired his death once! To-day the news gave her little satisfaction.

Mr. Wyatt took a slip of newspaper from his card-case, and read her the brief account of the Colonel's exit from this mortal strife. Duels were common enough at Hombourg in those days, and the journal made very little of the sanguinary business.

'As many of my friends believe me to have

been left a widow long ago I shall make no fuss
about this event; and I shall be very grateful if you
will be good enough not to talk of it anywhere,
Mrs. Walsingham said, by and by, after a thoughtful pause.

'I shall be careful to obey you,' answered the
lawyer.

'I wonder how you came to guess that I was not
a widow, and that Colonel Walsingham was my
husband? He took me abroad directly after our
marriage, and we were never in England together.'

'It is a solicitor's business to know a great many
things, and in this case there was a strong personal
interest. You accused me just now of flattering
women; and it is quite true that I have now and
then amused myself a little with the weaker of your
sex. Until about a year ago I believed myself
incapable of any real feeling, of any strong attachment, and had made up my mind to a life of solitude, relieved by the frivolities of society. But at that
time a marked change came over me, and I found
that I too was doomed to suffer life's great fever.

In a word, I fell desperately in love. I think you can guess the rest.'

'I am not very good at guessing, but I suppose the lady is some friend of mine, or you would scarcely choose me for a confidante. Is it Sophy Morton? I know you admire her.'

'As I admire wax dolls, or the Haydees and Zuleikas of an illustrated Byron,' answered Mr. Wyatt, with a wry face. 'Sophy Morton would have about as much power to touch my heart or influence my mind as the wax dolls or the Byronic beauties. There is only one woman I have ever loved, or ever can love, and her name is Clara Walsingham.'

Mrs. Walsingham looked at him with unaffected surprise.

'Of course I ought to feel very much flattered by such a declaration on your part, Mr. Wyatt, if I could quite bring myself to believe in your sincerity.'

'Put me to the proof.'

'I cannot do that. I can only thank you for the honour you have done me, and regret that you should endanger the smooth course of our friendship by that kind of declaration. I have learnt to rely upon you as a friend and an adviser, a thorough man of the world, and the last of mankind to lapse into sentimentality.'

'There is no sentimentality in the business, Mrs. Walsingham. I offer you a real and devoted affection, such an affection as a man feels but once in his life, and which a woman should scarcely reject without a thought of its value. I know I must seem at a disadvantage amongst the men who surround you, but they are men of the butterfly species, and I believe the best of them to be incapable of feeling as I feel for you. Yes, you are right when you call me a man of the world. It is to such men that love comes with its fullest force when it comes at all. I have not yielded weakly to the great master of mankind. I have counted the cost, and I know the devotion which I offer you to-day is as unalterable as it is profound.'

'I am sorry that I should have inspired any such sentiment, Mr. Wyatt. I can never return it.'

'Is that your irrevocable reply?'

'It is,' she answered, decisively.

'You reject the substance, an honest man's devoted love ; and yet you are content to waste the best years of your life upon a shadow.'

'I don't understand you.'

'Oh, yes, I think you do. I think you know as well as I do how frail a reed you have to lean on when you put your trust in Gilbert Sinclair.'

'You have no right to speak about Mr. Sinclair,' answered Clara Walsingham, with an indignant flush. 'What do you know of him, or of my feelings in relation to him ? '

'I know that you love him. Yes, Clara, it is the business of a friend to speak plainly, and even at the hazard of incurring your anger I will do so. Gilbert Sinclair is not worthy of your affection. You will know that I am right before long, if you do not know it now. It is not in that man's nature to be constant under difficulties, as I would be constant to you. Your hold upon him has been growing weaker every year.'

'If that is true I shall discover the fact quite soon enough from the gentleman himself,' replied Mrs. Walsingham, in a hard voice, and with an

angry cloud upon her face. 'Your friendship, as
you call it, is not required to enlighten me upon
a subject which scarcely comes within the province
of a confidential solicitor. Yes, Mr. Wyatt, since
plain speaking is to be the order of the day, I am
weak enough and blind enough to care for Gilbert
Sinclair, better than for any one else upon this
earth, and if I do not marry him I shall never
marry at all. He may intend to jilt me. Yes,
I have seen the change in him. It would be a
vain falsehood if I denied that. I have seen the
change, and I am waiting for the inevitable day in
which the man I once believed to be the soul of
truth shall declare himself a traitor.'

'Would it not be wise to take the initiative,
and give him his dismissal?'

'No. The wrong shall come from him. If he
can be base enough to forget all the promises of
the past, and to ignore the sacrifices I have made
for him, his infamy shall have no excuse from any
folly of mine.'

'And if you find that he is false to you—
that he has transferred his affection to another

woman—you will banish him from your heart and
mind, I trust, and begin life afresh.'

Mrs. Walsingham laughed aloud.

'Yes, I shall begin a new life, for from that
hour I shall only live upon one hope.'

'And that will be—— ?'

'The hope of revenge.'

'My dear Mrs. Walsingham——!' remonstrated
the lawyer.

'That sounds melodramatic, does it not?   But
you see there is a strong mixture of the melodramatic element in real life.   Gilbert Sinclair
should know that I am not a woman to be jilted
with impunity.   Of course I don't mean that I
should poison him, or stab him.   That sort of thing
is un-English and obsolete; except among the
labouring classes, who have a rapid way of taking
payment for the wrongs that are done them.   No;
I should not kill him, but rely upon it I should
make his life miserable.'

Mr. Wyatt watched her face with a thoughtful
expression in his own.   Yes, she looked the kind
of woman whose anger would take some tangible,

and perhaps fatal form. She was not a woman to carry the burden of a broken heart in silent patience to the grave.

'Upon my life I should be afraid to offend her,' thought James Wyatt.

'Revenge is a bad word,' he said, after another long pause. 'Redress is much better. If Mr. Sinclair should marry, as I have some reason to think he will——'

'What reason?'

'Public rumour. His attentions to a certain young lady have been remarked by people I know.'

'The lady is the beautiful Miss Clanyarde.'

'How did you discover that?'

'From his face, the other night.'

'You are quick at reading his face. Yes, I believe he is over head and ears in love with Constance Clanyarde, as a much better man, Cyprian Davenant, was before him; and I have no doubt Lord Clanyarde will do his utmost to bring the match about.'

'How long has this been going on?'

'Since the beginning of this season. He may

have lost his heart to the lady last year, but his
attentions last year were not so obvious.'

'Do you know if Miss Clanyarde cares for him ? '

'I have no means of knowing the lady's
feeling on the subject, but I have a considerable
knowledge of her father, in the way of business;
and I am convinced she will be made—induced
is, I suppose, a more appropriate word—to accept
Sinclair as a husband. Lord Clanyarde is as poor
as Job, and as proud as Lucifer. Yes, I think we
may look upon the marriage as a certainty. And
now, Mrs. Walsingham, remember that by whatever
means you seek redress I am your friend, and
shall hold myself ready to aid and abet you in
the exaction of your just right. You have
rejected me as a husband. You shall discover
how faithful I can be as an ally.'

'I don't quite understand the nature of the
alliance you propose. Do you mean you will
help me to come between that man and all hope
of domestic happiness ? You do not know how
merciless I could be if chance gave me the
power to punish Gilbert Sinclair's infidelity'

I know that he will deserve little compassion from you.'

'But from you? He has never injured you.'

'Do not be so sure of that. There are petty insults and trivial injuries that make up the sum of a great wrong. Gilbert Sinclair has not treated me well. I will not trouble you with the dry details of our business relations, but I have sufficient reasons for resentment, without reference to you. And now I will intrude upon you no longer. I see you are a little tired of this conversation. I only entreat you, once more, to remember that I am your friend.'

Mrs. Walsingham looked at him with a doubtful expression. He had subjugated her pride completely by the boldness of his attack. At another time she might have been angry with him, but the weariness of her spirit and the dull sense of impending sorrow were more powerful than anger. She only felt humiliated and perplexed by James Wyatt's proffers of love and friendship, uncertain how far he had been sincere in either offer.

I have no doubt I ought to be grateful to

you, Mr. Wyatt,' she said, in a slow weary way,
'but I do not think your friendship can ever
be of much service to me in the future business
of my life, and I trust that you will forget all
that has been said this morning. Good-bye.'

She gave him her hand. He held it with a
gentle pressure as he answered her,—

'It is impossible for me to forget anything
that you have said, but you shall find me as
secret as the grave. Good-bye.'

He bent his head, and touched her hand
lightly with his lips before releasing it. In the
next instant he was gone.

'How she loves that snob!' he said to himself as he walked away from Half-moon Street
'And how charming she is! Rich, too. I could
scarcely make a better match. It is a case in
which inclination and prudence go together.
And how easily I might have won her, but for
that man! Well, well, I don't despair of ultimate
victory, in spite of Gilbert Sinclair. "Time and
I against any two," as Philip of Spain used to
say when things went badly in the Netherlands.'

CHAPTER V.

'TIME IS, TIME WAS.'

MRS. WALSINGHAM wrote to Gilbert Sinclair, immediately after Mr. Wyatt's departure, a few hasty lines begging him to come to her without delay.

'Something has occurred,' she wrote, 'an event of supreme importance to me. I will tell you nothing more till we meet.'

She despatched her groom to the Albany with this note, and then waited with intense impatience for Gilbert Sinclair's coming. If he were at home it was scarcely possible he could refuse to come to her.

'I shall know the worst very soon,' she said to herself, as she sat behind the flowers that shaded her window. 'After to-day there shall be no uncertainty between us—no further reservation on my part—no more acting on his. He

shall find that I am not his dupe, to be fooled to
the top of my bent, and to be taken by surprise
some fine morning by the announcement of his
marriage in the *Times.*'

Mr. Sinclair was not at home when the note
was delivered, but between two and three o'clock
in the afternoon his thundering knock assailed the
door, and he came into the room unannounced.

In spite of the previous night's ball he had
ridden fifteen miles into the country that morning
to attend a sale of hunters, and was looking flushed
after his long ride.

'What on earth is the matter, Clara?' he asked.
'I have been out since eight o'clock. Poor Townley's
stud was sold off this morning at a pretty little
place he had beyond Barnet, and I rode down
there to see if there was anything worth bidding
for. I might have saved myself the trouble, for
I never saw such a pack of screws. The ride was
pleasant enough, however.'

'I wonder you were out so early after last
night's dance.'

'Oh, you've seen my name down among the

swells,' he answered, with a forced laugh. 'Yes, I was hard at it last night, no end of waltzes and galops. But you know late hours never make much difference to me.'

'Was it a very pleasant party?'

'The usual thing—too many people for the rooms.'

'Your favourite, Miss Clanyarde, was there, I see.'

'Yes, the Clanyardes were there. But I suppose you haven't sent for me to ask me questions about Lady Deptford's ball? I thought by your letter something serious had happened.'

'Something serious has happened. My husband is dead.'

She said the words very slowly, with her eyes fixed on Gilbert Sinclair's face. The florid colour faded suddenly out of his cheeks, and left him ghastly pale. Of all the events within the range of probability this was the last he had expected to hear of, and the most unwelcome.

'Indeed,' he stammered, after an awkward pause. 'I suppose I ought to congratulate you on the recovery of your freedom?'

'I am very glad to be free.'

'What did he die of—Colonel Walsingham?
And how did you get the news?'

'From a foreign paper. He was killed in a
duel.'

And then she repeated the contents of the paragraph James Wyatt had read to her.

'Is the news correct, do you think? No mistake about the identity of the person in question?'

'None whatever, I am convinced. However, I
shall drive into the City presently, and see the
solicitor who arranged our separation. I know the
Colonel was in the habit of corresponding with him,
and no doubt he will be able to give me official
intelligence of the event.'

After this there came another pause, more awkward than the first. Gilbert sat with his eyes
fixed upon the carpet, tracing out the figures of it
meditatively with the ferrule of his cane, with an
air of study as profound as if he had been an art
designer bent upon achieving some novel combi-
nation of form and colour. Clara Walsingham sat
opposite to him, waiting for him to speak, with a

pale, rigid face, that grew more stony as the silence continued. That silence became at last quite unendurable, and Gilbert felt himself obliged to say something, no matter what.

'Does this business make any alteration in your circumstances?' he asked, with a faint show of interest.

'Only for the better. I surrendered to the Colonel the income of one of the estates my father left me, in order to bribe him into consenting to a separation. Henceforward that income will be mine. My poor father took pains to secure me from the possibility of being ruined by a husband. My fortune was wholly at my own disposal, but I was willing to make the surrender in question in exchange for my liberty.'

'I am glad to find you will be so well off,' said Mr. Sinclair, still engrossed by the pattern of the carpet.

'Is that all you have to say?'

'What more can I say upon the subject?'

'There was a time when you would have said a great deal more.'

'Very likely,' answered Gilbert, bluntly; 'but then you see that time is past and gone. What is it Friar Bacon's brazen head said—"Time is, time was, time's past." Come, Clara, it is very little use for you and me to play at cross purposes. Why did you send for me in such hot haste to tell me of your husband's death?'

'Because I had reason to consider the news would be as welcome to you as it was to me.'

'That might have been so if the event had happened a year or two ago; unhappily your release comes too late for my welfare. You accused me the other day of intending to jilt you. I think that accusation scarcely fair, when it is remembered how long I was contented to remain your devoted slave, patiently waiting for something better than slavery. There is a limit to all things, however, and I confess the bondage became a little irksome at last, and I began to look in other directions for the happiness of my future life.'

'Does that mean that you are going to be married?'

'It does.'

'The lady is Miss Clanyarde, I conclude,' said Mrs. Walsingham. Her breathing was a little hurried, but there was no other sign of the storm that raged within.

'Yes, the lady is Constance Clanyarde. And now, my dear Clara, let me entreat you to be reasonable, and to consider how long I waited for the chance that has come at last too late to be of any avail, so far as I am concerned. I am not coxcomb enough to fear that you will regret me very much, and I am sure you know that I shall always regard you with the warmest friendship and admiration. With your splendid attractions you will have plenty of opportunities in the matrimonial line, and will have, I dare say, little reason to lament my secession.'

Clara Walsingham looked at him with unutterable scorn.

'And I once gave you credit for a heart, Gilbert Sinclair,' she said. 'Well, the dream is ended.'

'Don't let us part ill friends, Clara. Say you wish me well in my new life.'

'I cannot say anything so false. No, Gilbert,

I will not take your hand. There can be no such thing as friendship between you and me.'

'That seems rather hard,' answered Sinclair, in a sulky tone. 'But let it be as you please. Good-bye.'

'Good morning, Mr. Sinclair.'

Mrs. Walsingham rang the bell, but before her summons could be answered, Gilbert Sinclair had gone out of the house. He walked back to the Albany in a very gloomy frame of mind, thinking it a hard thing that Colonel Walsingham should have chosen this particular time for his death. He was glad that the interview was over, and that Clara knew what she had to expect; but he felt an uneasy sense that he had not altogether extricated himself from an awkward entanglement.

'She took it pretty quietly upon the whole,' he said to himself, 'but there was a look in her eyes that I didn't like.'

Mrs. Walsingham called on her late husband's lawyer in the course of the afternoon, and received a confirmation of James Wyatt's news. Her husband's death increased her income from two to three thousand a year, arising chiefly from landed property which had been purchased by her father, a city tradesman, who had late in life conceived the idea of becoming a country squire, and had died of the dulness incident upon an unrecognised position in the depths of an agricultural district. His only daughter's marriage with Colonel Walsingham had been a severe affliction to him, but he had taken care to settle his money upon her in such a manner as to secure it from any serious depredations on the part of the husband.

CHAPTER VI.

THE summer had melted into autumn, the London season was over, and the Clanyardes had left their furnished house in Eaton Place, which the Viscount had taken for the season, to return to Marchbrook, where Gilbert Sinclair was to follow them as a visitor. He had proposed for Constance, and had been accepted, with much inward rejoicing on the part of the lady's father; with a strange conflict of feeling in the mind of the lady herself.

Did she love the man she had promised to marry? Well, no, there was no such feeling as love for Gilbert Sinclair in her mind. She thought him tolerably good-looking, and not exactly disagreeable, and it had been impressed upon her that he was one of the richest men in England, a man who could bestow upon her everything which a well-bred young lady must, by nature and education, desire. The bitter pinch of poverty had been severely felt at Marchbrook, and the Clanyarde girls had been taught, in an indirect kind of way that they were bound to contribute to the restoration of the family fortunes by judicious marriages. The two elder girls, Adela and Margaret, had married well,—one Sir Henry Elrington, a Sussex baronet, with a very nice place, and a comfortable income, the other a rich East Indian merchant, considerably past middle age. But the fortunes of Sir Henry Elrington and Mr. Campion, the merchant, were as nothing compared with the wealth of Gilbert Sinclair; and Lord Clanyarde told his daughter Constance that she would put her sisters to shame by the brilliancy of her marriage. He flew into a terrible passion when she expressed herself disinclined to accept Mr. Sinclair's offer, and asked her how she dared to fly in the face of Providence by refusing such a splendid destiny. What in heaven's name did she expect? A girl without a sixpence of her own, and with nothing but her pretty face and aristocratic lineage to recommend her. Then came the two married

sisters with more lecturing and persuasion, and at
last the girl gave way, fairly wearied out, and
suffered herself to be scolded into a kind of des-
ponding submission.

So Gilbert Sinclair came one morning to Eaton
Place, and finding Miss Clanyarde alone in the
drawing-room, made her a solemn offer of his heart
and hand. He had asked her to be his wife before
this, and she had put him off with an answer that
was almost a refusal. Then had come the scolding
and lecturing, and she had been schooled into
resignation to a fate that seemed to her irresistible.
She told her suitor that she accepted him in
deference to her father's wishes, and that she could
give him nothing better than duty and gratitude
in return for the affection he was so good as to
entertain for her. This was enough for Gilbert,
who was bent on winning her for his wife, in a
headstrong, reckless spirit, that made no count
of the cost. He put down this speech of Constance's
to girlish modesty. She couldn't help being fond
of him, he thought, when he was so fond of her,
and such a good-looking fellow into the bargain.

He was not at all inclined to undervalue his own merits, or to suppose that any woman could feel indifferent to him. Had not Clara Walsingham loved him with an inconvenient devotedness? But as Miss Clanyarde sat by and by with her hand in her lover's, and listened to his protestations of affection, there rose before her the vision of a face that was not Gilbert Sinclair's—a darkly splendid face, that had looked upon her with such unutterable love one summer day in the shadowy Kentish lane; and she wished that Cyprian Davenant had carried her off to some strange, desolate land, in which they might have lived and died together.

'What will he think of me when he hears that I have sold myself to this man for the sake of his fortune?' she asked herself; and then she looked up at Gilbert's face and wondered whether she could ever teach herself to love him, or to be grateful to him for his love.

All this had happened within a week of Gilbert's final interview with Mrs. Walsingham, and in a very short time the fact of Mr. Sinclair's

engagement to Miss Clanyarde was pretty well
known to all that gentleman's friends and acquaintance.   He was very proud of carrying off a girl
whose beauty had made a considerable sensation
in the two past seasons, and he talked of his
matrimonial projects in a swaggering, boastful
way, that was eminently distasteful to some of his
acquaintance.   Men who were familiar with
Mr. Sinclair's antecedents shrugged their shoulders
ominously when his marriage was discussed, and
augured ill for the future happiness of Miss
Clanyarde.

James Wyatt was one of the first to congratulate him upon his betrothal.

'Yes,' answered Gilbert, 'she's a lovely girl, isn't
she? and of course I'm very proud of her affection.
It's to be a regular love match, you know.   I
wouldn't marry the handsomest woman in the
world if I thought she were marrying me for my
money.   I don't say the father hasn't an eye to
the main chance.   He's a thorough man of the
world, and of course fully alive to that kind of
thing.   But Constance is superior to any such

consideration. If I didn't believe that, I wouldn't be such a fool as to stake my happiness on the venture.'

'I scarcely fancied you would look at matters from such a sentimental point of view,' said Mr. Wyatt, thoughtfully, 'especially as this is by no means your first love.'

'It is the first love worth speaking of,' answered the other. 'I never knew what it was to be passionately in love till I met Constance Clanyarde.'

'Not with Mrs. Walsingham ?'

'No, Jim. I did care for her, a good deal, once upon a time, but never as I care for Constance. I think if that girl were to play me false I should kill myself. By the way, I'm sure you know more about Sir Cyprian Davenant than you were inclined to confess the other night. I fancy there was some kind of love affair—some youthful flirtation between him and Constance. You might as well tell me everything you know about it.'

'I know nothing about Miss Clanyarde, and I can tell you nothing about Davenant. He and I

are old friends, and I am too fully in his confidence
to talk of his sentiments, or his affairs.'

'What a confounded prig you are, Wyatt! But
you can't deny that Davenant was in love with
Constance. I don't believe she has ever cared a
straw for him, however, and if he should live to
come back to England I shall take good care he
never darkens my doors. How about that place
of his, by-the-bye? Is it in the market?'

'Yes, I have received Sir Cyprian's instructions
to sell whenever I see a favourable opportunity.
He won't profit much by the sale, poor fellow, for
the Davenant estate is mortgaged up to the
hilt.'

'I'll look at the place while I'm at Marchbrook,
and if I like it I may make you an offer. We shall
want something nearer town than the barrack my
father built in the north, but I shall not give up
that either.'

'You can afford a couple of country seats. You
will have a house in town, of course?'

'Yes, I have been thinking of Park Lane; but
it is so difficult to get anything there. I've told

the agents what I want, however, and I dare say they'll find something before long.'

'When are you to be married?'

'Not later than October, I hope. There is not the shadow of a reason for delay.'

At Marchbrook everything went pleasantly enough with the plighted lovers. Lord Clanyarde had filled the house with company, and his youngest daughter had very little time for reflection or regret upon the subject of her approaching marriage. Everybody congratulated her upon her conquest, and praised Gilbert Sinclair with such a show of enthusiasm that she began to think he must be worthy of a warmer regard than she was yet able to feel for him. She told herself that in common gratitude she was bound to return his affection, and she tried her utmost to please him by a ready submission to all his wishes; but the long drives and rides, in which they were always side by side, were very wearisome to her, nor could his gayest talk of the future, the houses, the yacht, the carriages and horses that were to be hers, inspired her with any expectation of happiness.

They rode over to Davenant with Lord Clanyarde one morning, and explored the old house, Gilbert looking at everything in a business-like spirit, which jarred a little upon Constance. She could not but remember that luckless exile who had loved the place so well.

Her lover consulted her about the disposition of the rooms, the colours of the new draperies, and the style of the furniture.

'We'll get rid of the gloomy old tapestry, and have everything modern and bright,' he said; but Lord Clanyarde pleaded hard for the preservation of the tapestry, which was very fine and in excellent condition.

'Oh, very well,' answered Gilbert, carelessly. 'In that case we'll keep the tapestry. I suppose the best plan will be to get some first-class London man to furnish the house. Those fellows always have good taste. But of course he must defer to you in all matters, Constance.'

'You are very good,' she returned, listlessly. 'But I don't think there will be any necessity for my interference.'

'Don't say that, Constance. That looks as if you were not interested in the subject,' Gilbert said, with rather a discontented air.

The listlessness of manner which his betrothed so often displayed was by no means pleasing to him. There was a disagreeable suspicion growing in his mind that Miss Clanyarde's heart had not quite gone with her acceptance of his offer, that family influences had something to do with her consent to become his wife. He was not the less resolved on this account to hold her to her promise; but his selfish tyrannical nature resented her coldness, and he was determined that the balance should be adjusted between them in the future.

'Perhaps you don't like this place, Constance,' he said presently, after watching her thoughtful face for some minutes in silence.

'Oh, yes, Gilbert, I am very fond of Davenant. I have known it all my life, you know.'

'Then I wish you'd look a little more cheerful about my intended purchase. I thought it would please you to have a country house so near your own family.'

'And it does please her very much, I am sure, Sinclair,' said Lord Clanyarde, with a stealthy frown at his daughter. 'She cannot fail to appreciate the kindness and delicacy of your choice.'

'Papa is quite right, Gilbert,' added Constance. 'I should be very ungrateful if I were not pleased with your kindness.'

After this she tried her utmost to sustain an appearance of interest in the discussion of furniture and decorations; but every now and then she found her mind wandering away to the banished owner of those rooms, and she wished that Gilbert Sinclair had chosen any other habitation upon this earth for her future home.

October came, and with it the inevitable day which was to witness one more perjury from the lips of a bride. The wedding took place at the little village church near Marchbrook, and was altogether a very brilliant affair, attended by all the relatives of the Clanyarde family, who were numerous, and by a great many acquaintances of bride and bridegroom. Notable among the friends of the latter was James Wyatt, the solicitor who had been employed in the drawing up of the marriage settlement, which was a most liberal one, and highly satisfactory to Viscount Clanyarde. Mr. Wyatt made himself excessively agreeable at the breakfast, and was amazingly popular among the bridesmaids. He did not long avail himself of the Marchbrook hospitalities, but went quietly back to town by rail almost immediately after the departure of the newly married couple on their honeymoon trip to the Italian lakes. He had an engagement in Half-moon Street that evening at eight o'clock.

The neighbouring clocks were striking the hour as he knocked at the door. Mrs. Walsingham was quite alone in the drawing-room, and looked unusually pale in the light of the lamps. The solicitor shook his head reproachfully as he pressed her hand.

'This is very sad,' he murmured, in a semi-paternal manner. 'You have been worrying yourself all day long, I know. You are as pale as a ghost.'

'I am a little tired, that is all.'

'You have been out to-day? You told me you should not stir from the house.'

'I changed my mind at the last moment. Anything was better than staying at home keeping the day like a black fast. Besides, I wanted to see how Gilbert and his bride would look at the altar.'

'You have been down to Kent?'

'Yes, I was behind the curtains of the organ loft. The business was easily managed by means of a sovereign to the clerk. I wore my plainest dress and a thick veil, so there was very little risk of detection.'

'What folly!' exclaimed Wyatt.

'Yes, it was great folly, no doubt, but it is the nature of women to be foolish. And now tell me all about the wedding. Did Gilbert look very happy?'

'He looked like a man who has got his own way, and who cares very little what price he has paid, or may have to pay, for the getting it.'

'And do you think he will be happy?'

'Not if his happiness depends upon the love of his wife.'

'Then you don't think she loves him?'

'I am sure she does not. I made a study of her face during the ceremony and afterwards; and if ever a woman sold herself, or was sold by her people, this woman is guilty of such a bargain.'

'Perhaps you say this to please me,' said Clara doubtfully.

'I do not, Mrs. Walsingham. I am convinced that this affair has been brought about by Lord Clanyarde's necessities, and not the young lady's choice. But I doubt whether this will make much difference to Gilbert in the long run. He is not a man of fine feelings, you know, and I think he will be satisfied with the fact of having won the woman he wanted to marry. I should fancy matters would go smoothly enough with him, so long as he sees no cause for jealousy. He would be rather an ugly customer if he took it into his head to be jealous.'

'And you think his life will go smoothly,' said Clara, 'and that he will go on to the end unpunished for his perfidy to me?'

'What good would his punishment be to you?'

'It would be all the world to me.'

'And if I could bring about the retribution you desire—if it were in my power to avenge your wrongs—what reward would you give me?'

She hesitated for a moment, knowing there was only one reward he was likely to claim from her.

'If you were a poor man I would offer you two-thirds of my fortune,' she said.

'But you know that I am not a poor man. If I can come to you some day, and tell you that Gilbert Sinclair and his wife are parted for ever, will you accept me for your husband?'

'Yes,' she answered, suddenly. 'Break the knot between those two—let me be assured that he has lost the woman for whose sake he jilted me, and I will refuse you nothing.'

'Consider it done. There is nothing in the world I would not achieve to win you for my wife.'

CHAPTER VII.

IT was not till the early spring that Mr. and Mrs
Sinclair returned to England. They had spent the
winter in Rome, where Gilbert had found some con-
genial friends, and where their time had been occupied
in one perpetual round of gaiety and dissipation.
Constance had shown a great taste for pleasure since
her marriage. She seemed to know no weariness of
visiting and being visited; and people who remembered her in her girlish days were surprised
to find what a thorough woman of the world she had
become. Nor was Gilbert displeased that it should
be so. He liked to see his wife occupy a prominent
position in society, and having no taste himself for
the pleasures of the domestic hearth, he was neither
surprised nor vexed by Constance's indifference to
her home. Of course it would all be different at
Davenant Park. There would be plenty of home

life there—a little too much, perhaps, Gilbert thought
with a yawn.

They had been married nearly four months,
and there had not been the shadow of disagreement
between them. Constance's manner to her husband
was amiability itself. She treated him a little *de
haut en bas* it is true, made her own plans for the
most part without reference to him, and graciously
informed him of her arrangements after they were
completed. But then, on the other hand, she never
objected to his disposal of his time, was never
exacting, or jealous, or capricious, as Clara Walsingham had been. She was always agreeable to
his friends, and was eminently popular with all of
them. So Gilbert Sinclair was, upon the whole, perfectly satisfied with the result of his marriage, and
had no fear of evil days in the future. What James
Wyatt had said of him was perfectly true. He was
not gifted with very fine feelings, and that sense of
something wanting in such a union, which would
have disturbed the mind of a nobler man, did not
trouble him.

They returned to England early in February,

and went at once to Davenant, which had been furnished in the modern mediæval style by a West End upholsterer. The staff of servants had been provided by Lady Elrington, who had come up to London on purpose, and had bestowed much pains and labour upon the task of selection, bitterly bewailing the degeneracy of the race she had to deal with during the performance of this difficult service. All was ready when Mr. and Mrs. Sinclair arrived. A pompous housekeeper simpered and curtseyed in the hall; an accomplished cook hovered tenderly over the roasts and the stew-pans in the great kitchen; housemaids in smart caps flitted about the passages and poked the fires in bedroom and dressing-rooms, bath-rooms and morning-room, eager to get an early look at their new lady; a butler of the usual clerical appearance ushered the way to the lamp-lit drawing-room, while two ponderous footmen conveyed the rugs and newspapers and morocco bags from the carriage, leaving all the heavier luggage to the care of unknown underlings attached to the stable department. Mr. and Mrs. Sinclair dined alone upon this first evening of their return, under the inspection of the clerical butler and the two ponderous footmen. They talked chiefly about the house, which rooms were most successful in their new arrangement, and so on ; a little about what they had been doing in Rome ; and a little about their plans for the next month ; what guests were to be invited, and what rooms they were to occupy. It was all the most conventional talk, but the three serving-men retired with the impression that Gilbert Sinclair and his wife were a very happy couple, and reported to that effect in the housekeeper's room and the servants' hall.

Before the week had ended the great house was full of company. That feverish desire for gaiety and change, which had seemed a part of Constance's nature since her marriage, in no way subsided on her arrival at Davenant. She appeared to exist for pleasure, and pleasure only, and her guests declared her the most charming hostess that ever reigned over a country house. Lavish as he was, Mr. Sinclair opened his eyes to their widest extent when he perceived his wife's capacity for spending money.

' It's rather lucky for you that you didn't marry

a poor man, Constance,' he said, with a boastful laugh.

She looked at him for a moment with a strange expression, and then turned very pale.

'I should not have been afraid to face poverty,' she said, 'if it had been my fate to do so.'

'If you could have faced it with the man you liked, eh, Constance? That's about what you mean, isn't it?'

'Is this intended for a complaint, Gilbert?' his wife asked, in her coldest tones. 'Have I been spending too much money?'

'No, no, I didn't mean that. I was only congratulating you upon your fitness for the position of a rich man's wife.'

This was the first little outbreak of jealousy of which Gilbert Sinclair had been guilty. He knew now that his wife did not love him, that his conquest had been achieved through the influence of her family, and he was almost angry with himself for being so fond of her. He could not forget those vague hints that had been dropped about Sir Cyprian Davenant, and was tormented by the idea

that James Wyatt knew a great deal more than he
had revealed upon this point. This hidden jealousy
had been at the bottom of his purchase of the
Davenant estate. He took a savage pride in
reigning over the little kingdom from which his
rival had been deposed.

Among the visitors from London appeared Mr.
Wyatt, always unobtrusive, and always useful. He
contrived to ingratiate himself very rapidly in Mrs.
Sinclair's favour, and established himself as a kind
of adjutant in her household corps, always ready
with advice upon every social subject, from the
costumes in a *tableau vivant* to the composition of
the *menu* for a dinner party. Constance did not
particluarly like him; but she lived in a world in
which it is not necessary to have a very sincere
regard for one's acquaintance; and she considered
him an agreeable person, much to be preferred to the
generality of her husband's chosen companions, who
were men without a thought beyond the hunting-
field and the racecourse.

Mr. Wyatt, on his part, was a little surprised to
see the manner in which Lord Clanyarde's daughter

filled her new position, the unfailing vivacity which she displayed in the performance of her duties as hostess, and the excellent terms upon which she appeared to live with her husband. He was accustomed, however, to look below the surface of things, and by the time he had been a fortnight at Davenant he had discovered that all this brightness and gaiety on the part of the wife indicated an artificial state of being, which was very far from real happiness, and that there was a growing sense of disappointment on the part of the husband.

He was not in the habit of standing upon much ceremony in his intercourse with Gilbert Sinclair, and on the first convenient occasion questioned him with blunt directness upon the subject of his marriage.

'I hope the alliance has brought you all the happiness you anticipated,' he said.

'Oh, yes, Jim,' Mr. Sinclair answered, rather moodily, 'my wife suits me pretty well. We get on very well together. She's a little too fond of playing the woman of fashion; but she'll get tired of that in time, I dare say. I'm fond of society myself, you

know, couldn't lead a solitary life for any woman in
Christendom ; but I should like a wife who seemed
to care a little more for my company, and was not
always occupied with other people. I don't think
we have dined alone a dozen times since we were
married.'

It was within a few days of this conversation
that Mr. Wyatt gratified himself by the performance
of a little experiment which he had devised in the
comfortable retirement of his bachelor room at
Davenant. He had come into Mrs. Sinclair's
morning-room after breakfast to consult her upon
the details of an amateur dramatic performance that
was to take place shortly, and had, for a wonder,
found the husband and wife alone together.

'Perhaps we'd better discuss the business at some
other time,' he said. 'I know Sinclair doesn't care
much about this sort of thing.'

'Is that your theatrical rubbish ?' asked Gilbert.
'You'd better say what you've got to say about it.
You needn't mind me. I can absorb myself in the
study of *Bell's Life* for a quarter of an hour or so.'

He withdrew to one of the windows, and read his

newspaper, while James Wyatt showed Constance
the books of some farces that had just come to him
by post, and discussed the fitness of each for
drawing-room representation.

'Every amateur in polite society believes himself
able to play Charles Mathews's business,' he said,
laughing. 'It is a fixed delusion of the human mind.
Of course we shall set them all by the ears, do what
we may. Perhaps it would be better to let them
draw lots for the characters, or we might put the
light comedy parts up to auction, and send the
proceeds to the poor box.'

He ran on in this strain gaily enough, writing
lists of the characters and pieces, and putting down
the names of the guests with a rapid pen as he talked,
until Gilbert Sinclair threw down his newspaper and
came over to the fireplace, politely requesting his
friend to 'stop that row.'

It was a hopelessly wet morning, and the master
of Davenant was sorely at a loss for amusement and
occupation. He had come to his wife's room in
rather a defiant spirit, determined that she should
favour him with a little more of her society than it

was her habit to give him, and he had found her
writing letters, which she declared were imperative,
and had sat by the fire waiting for her correspondence
to be finished, in a very sulky mood.

'What's the last news, Wyatt?' he asked, poking
the fire savagely.   'Anything stirring in London?'

'Nothing—in London.   There is some news of
an old friend of mine who's far away from London—
news I don't altogether like.'

'Some client who has bolted, in order to swindle
you out of a long bill of costs, I suppose,' answered
Gilbert, indifferently.

'No, the friend I am talking of is a gentleman
we all know—the late owner of this place.'

'Sir Cyprian Davenant?' cried Gilbert.

Constance looked up from her writing.

'Sir Cyprian Davenant,' repeated James Wyatt.

'Has anything happened to him?'

'About the last and worst thing that can happen
to any man, I fear,' answered the lawyer.   'For some
time since there have been no reports of Captain
Harcourt's expedition; and that, in a negative way,
was about as bad as it could be.   But in a letter I

received this morning, from a member of the
Geographical Society, there is worse news. My
friend tells me there is a very general belief that
Harcourt and his party have been made away with
by the natives. Of course this is only club gossip as
yet, and I trust that it may turn out a false alarm.'

Constance had dropped her pen, making a great
blot upon the page. She was very pale, and her
hands were clasped nervously upon the table before
her. Gilbert watched her with eager angry eyes. It
was just such an opportunity as he had wished for.
He wanted above all things to satisfy his doubts
about that man.

'I don't see that it much matters whether the
report is true or false,' he said, 'as far as Davenant
is concerned. The fellow was a scamp, and only
left England because he had spent his last sixpence
in dissipation.'

'I beg your pardon, Sinclair,' remonstrated Mr.
Wyatt, 'the Davenant property was impoverished by
Cyprian's father and grandfather. I don't say that
he was not extravagant himself at one period of his
life, but he had reformed long before he left England.'

'Reformed, yes, when he had no more money to
spend. That's a common kind of reform. However,
I suppose you've profited so much by his ruin that
you can afford to praise him.'

'Hadn't you better ring the bell?' asked James
Wyatt, quietly, 'I think Mrs. Sinclair has fainted.'

He was right, Constance Sinclair's head had
fallen back upon the cushion of her chair, and her
eyes were closed. Gilbert ran across to her, and
seized her hand. It was deadly cold.

'Yes,' he said, 'she has fainted. Sir Cyprian
was an old friend of hers. You know that better
than I do, though you have never chosen to tell me
the truth. And now, I suppose, you have trumped
up this story in order to let me see what a fool I
have been.'

'It is not a trumped-up story,' returned the other.
'It is the common talk amongst men who know the
travellers and their line of country.'

'Then for your friend's sake it is to be hoped it's
true.'

'Why so?'

'Because if he has escaped those black fellows to

come my way it will be so much the worse for both of us; for as sure as there is a sky above us, if he and I meet I shall kill him.'

'Bah!' muttered Mr. Wyatt, contemptuously, 'we don't live in the age for that sort of thing. Here comes your wife's maid; I'll get out of the way. Pray apologize to Mrs. Sinclair for my indiscretion in forgetting that Sir Cyprian was a friend of her family. It was only natural that she should be affected by the news.'

The lawyer went away as the maid came into the room. His face was brightened by a satisfied smile as he walked slowly along the corridor leading to the billiard-room.

' I think this fellow is made of the right kind of stuff for an Othello,' he said to himself. ' I've fired the train. If the news I heard is true, and Davenant is on his way home, there'll be nice work by and by.'

CHAPTER VIII.

GILBERT SINCLAIR said very little to his wife about the fainting fit. She was herself perfectly candid upon the subject. Sir Cyprian was an old friend—a friend whom she had known and liked ever since her childhood—and Mr. Wyatt's news had quite overcome her. She did not seem to consider it necessary to apologize for her emotion.

'I have been over-exerting myself a little lately, or I should scarcely have fainted, however sorry I felt,' she said quietly, and Gilbert wondered at her self-possession, but was not the less convinced that she had loved—that she did still love—Cyprian Davenant. He watched her closely after this to see if he could detect any signs of hidden grief, but her manner in society had lost none of its brightness ; and when the Harcourt expedition was next spoken of she bore her part in the conversation with perfect ease.

Mr. and Mrs. Sinclair left Davenant early in May for a charming house in Park Lane, furnished throughout with delicate tints of white and green, like a daisy-sprinkled meadow in early spring, a style in which the upholsterer had allowed full scope to the poetry of his own nature, bearing in mind that the house was to be occupied by a newly married couple. Mrs. Sinclair declared herself perfectly satisfied with the house, and Mrs. Sinclair's friends were in raptures with it. She instituted a Thursday evening supper after the opera, which was an immense success, and enjoyed a popularity in her new position of matron that excited some envy on the part of unmarried beauties. Mrs. Walsingham heard of the Thursday evening parties, and saw her beautiful rival very often at the opera ; but she heard from James Wyatt that Gilbert Sinclair spent a great deal of time at his club, and made a point of attending all the race meetings, habits that did not augur very well for his domestic happiness.

'He will grow tired of her, as he did of me,' thought Clara Walsingham.

But Gilbert was in no way weary of his wife. He

loved her as passionately as he had loved her at the first ; with an exacting and selfish passion, it is true, but with all the intensity of which his nature was capable.   If he had lived in the good old feudal days, when a man could do what he liked with his wife, he would have shut her up in some lonely turret, where no one but himself could approach her.   He knew that she did not love him; and with his own affection for her there was always mingled an angry sense of her coldness and ingratitude.

The London season came to an end once more, and Mr. and Mrs. Sinclair went back to Davenant. Nothing had been heard of Sir Cyprian or his companions throughout the summer, and Gilbert had ceased to trouble himself about his absent rival. The man was dead, in all probability, and it was something more than folly to waste a thought upon him. So things went on quietly enough, until the early spring gave a baby daughter to the master of Davenant, much to his disappointment, as he ardently desired a son and heir.

The birth of this infant brought a new sense of joy to the mind of Constance Sinclair.   She had not thought it possible that the child could give her so much happiness. She devoted herself to her baby with a tenderness which was at first very pleasing to her husband, but which became by and by distasteful to him. He grew jealous of the child's power to evoke so much affection from one who had never given him the love he longed for. The existence of his daughter seemed to bring him no nearer to his wife. The time and attention which she had given to society she now gave to her child ; but her husband was no more to her than he had ever been,— a little less perhaps, as he told himself angrily, in the course of his gloomy meditations.

Mrs. Walsingham read the announcement of the infant's birth, in extreme bitterness of spirit, and when James Wyatt next called upon her she asked him what had become of his promise that those two should be parted by his agency.

The lawyer shrugged his shoulders deprecatingly. 'I did not tell you that the parting should take place within any given time,' he said, 'but it shall go hard with me if I do not keep my promise sooner or later.

He had not been idle. The wicked work which

he had set himself to do had progressed considerably. It was he who always contrived, in a subtle manner, to remind Gilbert Sinclair of his wife's coldness towards her husband, and to hint at her affection for another, while seeming to praise and defend her. Throughout their acquaintance his wealthy client had treated him with a selfish indifference and a cool unconscious insolence that had galled him to the quick, and he took a malicious pleasure in the discomfiture which Sinclair had brought upon himself by his marriage. When the Sinclairs returned to London, some months after the birth of the child, James Wyatt contrived to make himself more than ever necessary to Gilbert, who had taken to play higher than of old, and who now spent four evenings out of the six lawful days at a notorious whist club, sitting at the card-table till the morning sun shone through the chinks in the shutters. Mr. Wyatt was a member of the same club, but too cautious a player for the set which Gilbert now affected.

'That fellow is going to the bad in every way,' the lawyer said to himself. 'If Clara Walsingham wants to see him ruined she is likely to have her wish without any direct interference of mine.'

The state of affairs in Park Lane was indeed far from satisfactory. Gilbert had grown tired of playing the indulgent husband, and the inherent brutality of his nature had on more than one occasion displayed itself in angry disputes with his wife, whose will he now seemed to take a pleasure in thwarting, even in trifles. He complained of her present extravagance, with insolent reference to the poverty of her girlhood, and asked savagely if she thought his fortune could stand for ever against her expensive follies.

'I don't think my follies are so likely to exhaust your income as your increasing taste for horse-racing, Gilbert,' she answered, coolly. 'What is to be the cost of these racing stables you are building near Newmarket? I heard you, and that dreadful man your trainer, talking of the tan gallop the other day and it seemed to me altogether rather an expensive affair, especially as your horses have such a knack of getting beaten. It is most gentlemanlike of you to remind me of my poverty. Yes, I was very poor in my girlhood,—and very happy.'

'And since you've married me you've been miserable. Pleasant, upon my soul! You'd have married that fellow Cyprian Davenant'and lived in a ten-roomed house in the suburbs, with a maid of all work to wait upon you, and called that happiness, I suppose?'

'If I had married Sir Cyprian Davenant I should at least have been the wife of a gentleman,' replied Constance.

This was not the first time that Gilbert had mentioned Cyprian Davenant of late. A report of the missing travellers had appeared in one of the newspapers, and their friends began to hope for their safe return. Gilbert Sinclair brooded over this probable return in a savage frame of mind, but did not communicate his thoughts on the subject to his usual confidant, Mr. Wyatt, who thereupon opined that those thoughts were more than ordinarily bitter.

Before the London season was over Mr. Sinclair had occasion to attend a rather insignificant meeting in Yorkshire where a two-year-old filly, from which he expected great things in the future, was to try her strength in a handicap race. He came home by way of Newmarket, where he spent a few days pleasantly enough in the supervision of his new buildings, and he had been absent altogether a week when he returned to Park Lane.

It was about four o'clock in the afternoon when he drove up to his own house in a hansom. He found his wife in the drawing-room, occupied with several visitors, amongst whom appeared a tall figure which he remembered only too well. It was Sir Cyprian Davenant, bronzed with travel, and looking handsomer than when he left London.

Gilbert stood at gaze for a moment, confounded by the surprise, and then went through the ceremony of handshaking with his wife's guests in a somewhat embarrassed manner.

Constance received him with her usual cool politeness, and he felt himself altogether at a disadvantage in the presence of the man he feared and hated. He seated himself, however, determined to see the end of this obnoxious visit, and remained moodily silent until the callers had dropped off one by one, Sir Cyprian among the earliest departures.

Gilbert turned savagely upon his wife directly the room was clear.

'So your old favourite has lost no time in re-
newing his intimacy with you,' he said. 'I came
home at rather an awkward moment, I fancy.'

'I did not perceive any particular awkwardness
in your return,' his wife answered, coolly, 'unless it
was your own manner to my friends, which was a
little calculated to give them the idea that you
scarcely felt at home in your own house.'

'There was some one here who seemed a little
too much at home, Mrs. Sinclair; some one who will
find my presence a good deal more awkward if I
should happen to find him here again. In plain
words, I forbid you to receive Sir Cyprian Davenant
in my house.'

'I can no more close my doors upon Sir Cyprian
Davenant than on any other visitor,' replied Constance, 'and I do not choose to insult an old friend
of my family for the gratification of your senseless
jealousy.'

'Then you mean to defy me?'

'There is no question of defiance. I shall do
what I consider right, without reference to this
absurd fancy of yours. Sir Cyprian is not very likely

to call upon me again, unless you cultivate his acquaintance.'

' I am not very likely to do that,' Gilbert answered, savagely. His wife's tranquillity baffled him, and he could find nothing more to say for himself. But this jealousy of Sir Cyprian was in no manner abated by Constance's self-possession. He remembered the fainting fit in the morning-room at Davenant, and he was determined to find some means of punishing her for her secret preference for this man. An ugly notion flashed across his mind by and by as he saw her with her child lying in her lap, bending over the infant with a look of supreme affection.

' She can find love for everything in the world except me,' he said to himself, bitterly. He had ceased to care for the child after the first month or so of its existence, being inclined to resent its sex as a personal injury, and feeling aggrieved by his wife's devotion to the infant, which seemed to make her indifference to himself all the more obvious.

He left the house when Constance went out for her daily drive in the park, and strolled in the same direction, caring very little where he went upon this

particular afternoon. The Ladies' Mile was thronged
with carriages, and there was a block at the Corner
when Gilbert took his place listlessly among the loun-
gers who were lolling over the rails. He nodded to the
men he knew, and answered briefly enough to some
friendly inquiries about his luck in Yorkshire.

'The filly ran well enough,' he said, 'but I doubt
if she's got stay enough for the Chester.'

'Oh, of course you want to keep her dark, Sinclair. I heard she was a flyer, though.'

Mr. Sinclair did not pursue the conversation.
The carriages moved on for a few paces, at the insti-
gation of a mounted policeman, and then stopped
again, leaving a perfectly appointed miniature
brougham exactly in front of Gilbert Sinclair. The
occupant of the brougham was Mrs. Walsingham.
The stoppage brought her so close to Gilbert that
it was impossible to avoid some kind of greeting.
The widow's face paled as she recognised Gilbert,
and then with a sudden impulse she held out her
hand. It was the first time they had met since that
unpleasant interview in Half-moon Street. The
opportunity was very gratifying to Mrs. Walsingham.

She had most ardently desired to see how Gilbert supported his new position, to see for herself how far Mr. Wyatt's account of him might be credited. She put on the propitiatory manner of a woman who has forgiven all past wrongs.

'Why do you never come to see me ? ' she asked.

'I scarcely thought you would care to receive me, after what you said when we last met,' he replied, rather embarrassed by her easy way of treating the situation.

'Let that be forgotten. It is not fair to remember what a woman says when she is in a passion. I think you expressed a wish that we might be friends after your marriage, and I was too angry to accept that proof of your regard as I should have done. I have grown wiser with the passage of time; and, believe me, I am still your friend.'

There was a softness in her tone which flattered and touched Gilbert Sinclair. It contrasted so sharply with the cool contempt he had of late suffered at the hands of his wife. He remembered how this woman had loved him; and he asked himself what good he had gained by his marriage with

Constance Clanyarde; except the empty triumph of an alliance with a family of superior rank to his own, and the vain delight of marrying an acknowledged beauty.

Before Mrs. Walsingham's brougham had moved on he had promised to look in upon her that evening, and at ten o'clock he was seated in the familiar drawing-room, telling her his domestic wrongs, and freely confessing that his marriage had been a failure. Little by little she beguiled him into telling her these things, and played her part of adviser and consoler with exquisite tact, not once allowing him to perceive the pleasure his confession afforded her. He spoke of his child without the faintest expression of affection, and laughed bitterly as he described his wife's devotion to her infant.

'I thought as a woman of fashion she would have given herself very little trouble about the baby,' he said, 'but she contrives to find time for maternal raptures in spite of her fashionable friends. I have told her that she is killing herself, and the doctors tell her pretty much the same; but she will have her own way.'

'She would suffer frightfully if the child were to die,' said Mrs. Walsingham.

'Suffer! Yes, I was thinking of that this afternoon when she was engaged in her baby-worship. She would take my death coolly enough, I have no doubt, but I believe the loss of that child would kill her.'

Long after Gilbert Sinclair had left her that night Clara Walsingham sat brooding over all that he had told her upon the subject of his domestic life.

'And so he has found out what it is to have a wife ·who does not care for him,' she said to herself. 'He has gratified his fancy for a lovely face, and is paying a heavy price for his conquest. And I am to leave all my hopes of revenge to James Wyatt, and am to reward his services by marrying him? No, no, Mr. Wyatt! It was all very well to promise that in the day of my despair. I see my way to something better than that now. The loss of her child would kill her, would it? And her death would bring Gilbert back to me, I think. His loveless marriage has taught him the value of a woman's affection.'

CHAPTER IX.

THE BEGINNING OF SORROW.

SIR CYPRIAN did not again call at the house in Park Lane. He had heard of Constance Clanyarde's marriage during his African travels, and had come back to England resolved to avoid her as far as it was possible for him to do so. Time and absence had done little to lessen his love, but he resigned himself to her marriage with another as an inevitable fact, only regretting she had married a man of whom he had by no means an exalted opinion. James Wyatt was one of the first persons he visited on his arrival in London, and from him he heard a very unsatisfactory account of the marriage. It was this that had induced him to break through his resolution and call in Park Lane. He wanted to see for himself whether Constance was unhappy. He saw little, however, to enlighten him on this point. He found the girl he had so fondly loved transformed into a perfect woman of the world; and he could draw no inference from her careless gaiety of manner, except that James Wyatt had said more than was justified by the circumstances of the case.

Instead of returning to Davenant for the autumn months, Mr. Sinclair chose this year to go to Germany; an extraordinary sacrifice of inclination one might suppose, as his chief delight was to be found at English race meetings, and in the supervision of his stable at Newmarket.

Mrs. Sinclair's doctor had recommended change of some kind as a cure for a certain lowness of tone, and general derangement of the nervous system under which his patient laboured. The medical man suggested Harrogate or Buxton— or some Welsh water-drinking place,—but when Gilbert proposed Schönesthal, in the Black Forest, he caught at the idea.

'Nothing could be better for Mrs. Sinclair and the baby,' he said, 'and you'll be near Baden-Baden if you want gaiety.'

'I don't care about brass bands and a lot
of people,' answered Gilbert. 'I can shoot caper-
cailzies. I shall get on well enough for a month
or so.'

Constance had no objection to offer to this
plan. She cared very little where her life was
spent, so long as she had her child with her.
A charming villa had been found, half hidden
among pine trees, and here Mr. Sinclair established his wife, with a mixed household of
English and foreign servants. She was very
glad to be so completely withdrawn from the
obligations of society, and to be able to devote
herself almost entirely to the little girl, who was
of course a paragon of infantine grace and intelligence in the eyes of mother and nurse. The
nurse was a young woman belonging to the village
near Marchbrook, one of the pupils of the
Sunday school, whom Constance had known from
girlhood. The nursemaid who shared her duties
n London had not been brought to Schönesthal,
but in her place Mrs. Sinclair engaged a French
girl, with sharp dark eyes, and a very intelli-

gent manner. Martha Briggs, the nurse, was rather more renowned for honesty and good temper than for intellectual qualifications, and she seemed unusually slow and stolid in comparison with the vivacious French girl. This girl had come to Baden with a Parisian family, and had been dismissed with an excellent character upon the family's departure for Vienna with a reduced staff. Her name was Melanie Duport, and she contrived very rapidly to ingratiate herself with her mistress, as she had done with the good priest of the little church she had attended during her residence at Baden, who was delighted with her artless fervour and unvarying piety. Poor Martha Briggs was rather inclined to be jealous of this new rival in her mistress's favour, and derived considerable comfort from the fact that the baby did not take kindly to Melanie.

If the baby preferred her English nurse to Melanie, the little French girl, for her part, seemed passionately devoted to the baby. She was always eager to carry the child when the two nurses were out together, and resented Martha's determination to deprive her of this pleasure. One day when the two were disputing together upon this subject, Martha bawling, at the French girl, under the popular delusion that she would make herself understood if she only talked loud enough, Melanie repeating her few words of broken English with many emphatic shrugs and frowns and nods, a lady who was strolling along the forest path, while her carriage waited for her at a little distance, stopped to listen to them, and to admire the baby. She spoke in French to Melanie, and did not address Martha at all, much to that young person's indignation. She asked Melanie to whom the child belonged, and how long she had been with it, and whether she was accustomed to nursing children, adding, with a smile, that she looked rather too ladylike for a nurse-maid.

Melanie was quite subdued by this compliment. She told the lady that this was the first time she had been nursemaid. She had been lady's-maid in her last situation, and had preferred the place very much to her present position. She told this strange lady nothing about that rapturous affection for the baby which she was in the habit of expressing in Mrs. Sinclair's presence. She only told her how uncomfortable she had been made by the English nurse's jealousy.

' I am staying at the Hôtel du Roi,' said the lady, after talking to Melanie for some little time, 'and should like to see you if you can find time to call upon me some evening. I might be able to be of some use to you in finding a new situation when your present mistress leaves the neighbourhood.'

Melanie curtseyed, and replied that she would make a point of waiting upon the lady, and then the two nurses moved on with their little charge. Martha asked Melanie what the foreign lady had been saying, and the French girl replied carelessly that she had only been praising the baby.

' And well she may,' answered Miss Briggs, rather snappishly, 'for she's the sweetest child that ever lived; but for my own part I don't like foreigners, or any of their nasty deceitful ways.'

This rather invidious remark was lost upon Mademoiselle Duport, who only understood a few words of English, and who cared very little for her fellow-servant's opinion upon any subject.

In spite of Gilbert Sinclair's protestation of indifference to the attractions of brass bands and crowded assemblies, he contrived to spend the greater part of his time at Baden, where the Goddess of Chance was still being worshipped in the brilliant Kursaal, while his wife was left to drink her fill of forest beauty, and that distant glory of inaccessible hills which the sun dyed rosy-red in the quiet eventide.

In these tranquil days, while her husband was waiting for the turn of Fortune's wheel in the golden *salon*, or yawning over "Galignani" in the reading-room, Constance's life came far nearer happiness than she had ever dared to hope it could come, after her perjury at God's altar two years ago. Many a time, while she was leading her butterfly life in the flower-garden of fashion, making dissipation stand for pleasure, she had told herself, in some gloomy hour of reaction, that no good ever could come of her marriage; that there was a curse upon it, a righteous God's anathema against falsehood. And then her baby had come, and she had shed her first happy tears over the sweet small face, the blue eyes looking up at her full of vague wonder, and she had thanked Heaven for this new bliss, and believed her sin forgiven. After that time Gilbert had changed for the worse, and there had been many a polite passage-at-arms between husband and wife, and these encounters, however courteously performed, are apt to leave ugly scars.

But now, far away from all her frivolous acquaintance, free from the all-engrossing duties of a fine lady's existence, she put all evil thoughts out of her mind, Gilbert amongst them, and abandoned herself wholly to the delight of the pine forest and baby. She was very gracious to Gilbert, when he chose to spend an hour or two at home, or to drive with her in the pretty little pony-carriage in which she made most of her explorations, but she made no complaint about his long absences, she expressed no curiosity as to the manner in which he amused himself, or the company he kept at Baden-Baden; and though that centre of gaiety was only four miles off, she never expressed a wish to share in its amusements.

Gilbert was not an agreeable companion at this time. That deep and suppressed resentment against his wife, like rancorous Iago's jealousy, did 'gnaw him inwards;' and although his old passionate love still remained, it was curiously interwoven with hatred.

Once when husband and wife were seated opposite each other in the September twilight after one of their rare *tête-à-tête* dinners, Constance looked up suddenly and caught Gilbert's brooding eyes fixed upon her face with an expression which made her shiver.

'If you look at me like that, Gilbert,' she said, with a nervous laugh, 'I shall be afraid to drink this glass of Chambertin you've just poured out for me. There might be poison in it. I hope I have done nothing to deserve such an angry look. Othello must have looked something like that, I should think, when he asked Desdemona for the strawberry-spotted handkerchief.'

'Why did you marry me, Constance ?' asked Sinclair, ignoring his wife's speech.

There was something almost piteous in this question, wrung from a man who loved honestly, according to his lights, and whose love was turned to rancour by the knowledge that it had won no return.

'What a question after two years of married life! Why did I marry you? Because you wished me to marry you, and because I believed you would make me a good husband, Gilbert, and because I had firmly resolved to make you a good wife.'

She said this earnestly, looking at him through her tears. Since her own life had become so much happier, since her baby's caresses had awakened all the dormant tenderness of her nature, she had felt more anxious to be on good terms with her husband. She would have taken much trouble—made some sacrifice of womanly pride—to win him back to that amiable state of mind she remembered in their honeymoon.

'I've promised to meet Wyatt at the Kursaal this evening,' said Sinclair, looking at his watch as he rose from the table, and without the slightest notice of his wife's reply.

'Is Mr. Wyatt at Baden?'

'Yes, he has come over for a little amusement at the tables—deuced lucky dog—always contrives to leave off a winner. One of those cool-headed fellows who know the turn of the tide. You've no objection to his being there, I suppose?'

'I wish you and he were not such fast friends, Gilbert. Mr. Wyatt is no favourite of mine.'

'Isn't he? Too much of the watch-dog about him, I suppose. As for fast friends, there's not much friendship between Wyatt and me. He's a useful fellow to have about one, that's all. He has served me faithfully, and has got well paid for his services. It's a matter of pounds, shillings, and pence on his side, and a matter of convenience on mine. No doubt Wyatt knows that as well as I do.'

'Don't you think friendship on such a basis may be rather an insecure bond?' said Constance, gravely, 'and that a man who can consent to profess friendship upon such degrading terms is likely to be half an enemy.'

'Oh, I don't go in for such high-flown ethics.

Jim Wyatt knows that it's his interest to serve me well, and that it's as much as his life is worth to play me false. Jim and I understand one another perfectly, Constance, you may be sure.'

'I am sure that he understands you,' answered Constance.

But Gilbert was gone before she had finished her sentence.

Baby, christened Christabel after the late Lady Clanyarde, was nearly a twelvemonth old, and had arrived, in the opinion of mother and nurse, at the most interesting epoch of babyhood. Her tender cooings, her joyous chucklings, her pretty cluck-clucking noises, as of anxious maternal hens calling their offspring, her inarticulate language of broken syllables, which only maternal love could interpret, made an inexhaustible fountain of delight. She was the blithest and happiest of babies, and every object in creation with which she became newly acquainted was a source of rapture to her. The flowers, the birds, the insect life of that balmy pine forest filled her with delight. The soft blue eyes sparkled with pleasure, the rosebud lips babbled

her wordless wonder, the little feet danced with
ecstasy.

'Oh,' cried the delighted mother, 'if she could
always be just like this, my plaything and my
darling ! Of course I shall love her just as dearly
when she is older—a long-armed lanky girl, in a
brown holland pinafore, always inking her fingers
and getting into trouble about her lessons—like my
sisters and me when we were in the schoolroom ;
but she can never be so pretty or so sweet again,
can she, Martha ? '

'Lor, 'mum, she'll always be a love,' replied
the devoted nurse ; 'and as for her arms being long
and her fingers inky, you won't love her a bit less
—and I'm sure I hope she won't be worried with
too many lessons, for I do think great folks'
children are to be pitied, half their time cooped up
in school-rooms, or stretched out on back-boards, or
strumming on the piano, while poor children are
running wild in the fields.'

'Oh, Martha, how shocking!' cried Mrs. Sinclair, pretending to be horrified, 'to think that one of my favourite pupils should underrate the value of education ! '

'Oh, no, indeed, ma'am, I have no such thought. I have often felt what a blessing it is to be able to read a good book and write a decent letter. But I never can think that life was meant to be all education.'

'Life is all education, Martha,' answered her mistress, with a sigh, 'but not the education of grammars and dictionaries. The World is our school, and Time our schoolmaster. No, Martha, my Christabel shall not be harassed with too' much learning. We won't try to make her a paragon. Her life shall be all happiness and freedom, and she shall grow up without the knowledge of care or evil, except the sorrows of others, and those she shall heal; and she shall marry the man she loves, whether he is rich or poor, for I am sure my sweet one would never love a bad man.'

'I don't say that, ma'am,' remarked Martha, 'looks are so deceiving. I'm sure, there was my own cousin, on the father's side, Susan Tadgers, married the handsomest young man in Marchbrook village, and before they'd been two years married he took to drinking, and was so neglectful of himself, you wouldn't have known him; and now she's gone back to her friends, and his whiskers, that he used to take such a pride in, are rusty-brown and shaggy, like a stray Scotch terrier.'

Three days after that somewhat unpleasant *tête-à-tête* between husband and wife Gilbert Sinclair announced his intention of going back to England for the Leger.

'I never have missed a Leger,' he said, as if attendance at that race were a pious duty, like the Commination service on Ash Wednesday, 'and I shouldn't like to miss this race.'

'Hadn't we better go home at once then, Gilbert? I am quite ready to return.'

'Nonsense! I've taken this place till the 20th of October, and shall have to pay pretty stiffly for it. I shall come back directly after the Doncaster.'

'But it will be a fatiguing journey for you.'

'I'd just as soon be sitting in a railway train as anywhere else.'

'Does Mr. Wyatt go back with you?'

'No, Wyatt stays at Baden for the next week or so. He pretends to be here for the sake of the waters, goes very little to the Kursaal, and lives quietly, like a careful old bachelor who wishes to mend a damaged constitution : but I should rather think he had some deeper game than water-drinking.'

Gilbert departed, and Constance was alone with her child. The weather was delightful, cloudless skies, balmy days : blissful weather for the grape-gatherers on the vine-clad slopes that sheltered one side of this quaint old village of Schönes-thal. A river wound through the valley, a deep and rapid stream narrowing in this cleft of the hills, and utilized by some saw-mills in the out-skirts of the village, whence at certain seasons rafts of timber were floated down the Rhine.

A romantic road following the course of this river was one of Mrs. Sinclair's favourite drives. There were picturesque old villages and mediæval ruins to be explored, and many lovely spots to be shown to baby, who, although inarticulate, was supposed to be appreciative.

Upon the first day of Gilbert's absence Martha Briggs came home from her afternoon promenade looking flushed and tired, and complaining of sore throat. Constance was quick to take alarm. The poor girl was going to have a fever, perhaps, and must instantly be separated from baby. There was no medical man nearer than Baden, so Mrs. Sinclair sent the groom off at once to that town. She told him to inquire for the best English doctor in the place, or if there were no English practitioner at Baden, for the best German doctor. The moment she had given these directions, however, it struck her that the man, who was not remarkable for intelligence out of his stable, was likely to lose time in making his inquiries, and perhaps get misdirected at last.

'Mr. Wyatt is at Baden,' she thought. 'I dare say he would act kindly in such an extremity as this, though I have no opinion of his sincerity in a general way. Stop, Dawson,' she said to the groom, 'I'll give you a note for Mr. Wyatt, who is staying at the Badenscher Hof. He will direct you to the doctor. You'll drive to Baden in the pony carriage, and if possible bring the doctor back with you.

Baby was transferred to the care of Melanie
Duport, who seemed full of sympathy and kindli-
ness for her fellow-servant, a sympathy which
Martha Briggs' surly British temper disdained.
Mrs. Sinclair had Martha's bed moved from the
nursery into her own dressing-room, where she
would be able herself to take care of the invalid.
Melanie was ordered to keep strictly to her nurseries,
and on no account to enter Martha's room.

'But if Martha has a fever, and Madame
nurses her, this little angel may catch the fever
from Madame,' suggested Melanie.

'If Martha's illness is contagious I shall not
nurse her,' answered Constance. 'I can get a
nursing sister from one of the convents. But I
like to have the poor girl near me, that, at the
worst, she may know she is not deserted.'

'Ah, but Madame is too good! What happiness to serve so kind a mistress!'

Mr. Wyatt showed himself most benevolently
anxious to be useful on receipt of Mrs. Sinclair's
note. He made all necessary inquiries at the office
of the hotel, and having found out the name of

the best doctor in Baden, took the trouble to accompany the groom to the medical man's house, and waited until Mr. Paulton, the English surgeon, was seated in the pony carriage.

'I shall be anxious to know if Mrs. Sinclair's nurse is seriously ill,' said Mr. Wyatt while the groom was taking his seat. 'I shall take the liberty to call at your surgery and inquire in the course of the evening.'

'Delighted to give you any information,' replied Mr. Paulton, graciously; 'I'll send you a line if you like. Where are you staying?'

'At the Badenscher.'

'You shall know how the young woman is directly I get back.'

'A thousand thanks.'

CHAPTER X.

THE CRUEL RIVER.

Mrs. SINCLAIR's precautions had been in no wise futile. Mr. Paulton pronounced that Martha's symptoms pointed only too plainly to scarlet fever. There could not be too much care taken to guard against contagion. The villa was airy and spacious, and Mrs. Sinclair's dressing-room at some distance from the nursery. There would be no necessity, therefore, Mr. Paulton said, for the removal of the child to another house. He would send a nursing sister from Baden—an experienced woman—to whose care the sick room might be safely confided.

The sister came—a middle-aged woman—in the sombre garb of her order, but with a pleasant, cheerful face, that well became her snow-white head-gear. She showed herself kind and dexterous in nursing the sick girl, but before she had been three days in the house Martha, who was now in a raging fever, took a dislike to the nurse, and raved wildly about this black-robed figure at her bedside. In vain did the sister endeavour to reassure her. To the girl's wandering wits that foreign tongue seemed like the gibberish of some unholy goblin. She shrieked for help, and Mrs. Sinclair ran in from the adjoining room to see what was amiss. Martha was calmed and comforted immediately by the sight of her mistress ; and from that time Constance devoted herself to the sick room, and shared the nurse's watch.

This meant separation from Christabel, and that was a hard trial for the mother who had never yet lived a day apart from her child ; but Constance bore this bravely for the sake of the faithful girl— too thankful that her darling had escaped the fever which had so strangely stricken the nurse. The weather continued glorious, and baby seemed quite happy with Melanie, who roamed about with her charge all day, or went for long drives in the pony carriage under the care of the faithful Dawson, who was a pattern of sobriety and steadiness, and incapable of flirtation.

Mr. Wyatt rode over from Baden every other day
to inquire about the nurse's progress—an inquiry
which he might just as easily have made of the
doctor in Baden,—and this exhibition of good
feeling on his part induced Constance to think
that she had been mistaken in her estimate of his
character.

'The Gospel says "judge not,"' she thought, 'and
yet we are always sitting in judgment upon one
another. Perhaps, after all, Mr. Wyatt is as kind-
hearted as his admirers think him, and I have done
wrong in being prejudiced against him. He was
Cyprian's friend, too, and always speaks of him with
particular affection.'

Constance remembered that scene in the morning-
room at Davenant. It was one of those unpleasant
memories which do not grow fainter with the
passage of years. She had been inclined to suspect
James Wyatt of a malicious intention in his sudden
announcement of Sir Cyprian's death—the wish to
let her husband see how strong a hold her first love
still had upon her heart. He, who had been Cyprian
Davenant's friend and confidant, was likely to have

known something of that early attachment, or at least to have formed a shrewd guess at the truth.

'Perhaps I have suspected him wrongly in that affair,' Constance thought, now that she was disposed to think more kindly of Mr. Wyatt. 'His mention of Sir Cyprian might have been purely accidental.'

Four or five times in every day Melanie Duport brought the baby Christabel to the grass-plat under the window of Mrs. Sinclair's bedroom, and there were tender greetings between mother and child, baby struggling in nurse's grasp, and holding up her chubby arms as if she would fain have embraced her mother, even at that distance. These interviews were a sorry substitute for the long happy hours of closest companionship which mother and child had enjoyed at Schönesthal, but Constance bore the trial bravely. The patient was going on wonderfully well, Mr. Paulton said; the violence of the fever was considerably abated. It had proved a lighter attack than he had apprehended. In a week the patient would most likely be on the high road to recovery, and then Mrs. Sinclair could leave her entirely to the Sister's care, since poor Martha was now restored to her right mind; and was quite reconciled to that trustworthy attendant.

'And then,' said Mr. Paulton, 'I shall send you to Baden for a few days, before you go back to baby, and you must put aside the clothes that you have worn in the sick room, and I think we shall escape all risk of infection.'

This was a good hearing. Constance languished for the happy hour when she should be able to clasp that rosy babbling child to her breast once more. Melanie Duport had been a marvel of goodness throughout this anxious time.

'I shall never forget how kind and thoughtful you have been, Melanie,' said Constance from her window, as the French girl stood in the garden below, holding baby up to be adored before setting out for her morning ramble.

'But it is a pleasure to serve Madame,' shrieked Melanie, in her shrill treble.

'Monsieur returns this evening,' said Constance, who had just received a hurried scrawl from Gilbert, naming the hour of his arrival, 'you must take care that Christabel looks her prettiest.'

'Ah, but she is always ravishingly pretty. If she were only a boy Monsieur would idolize her.'

'Where are you going this morning, Melanie?'

'To the ruined castle on the hill.'

'Do you think that is a safe place for baby?'

'What could there be safer? What peril can Madame foresee?'

'No,' said Constance, with a sigh. 'I suppose she is as safe there as anywhere else, but I am always uneasy when she is away from me.'

'But the love of Madame for this little one is a passion!'

Melanie departed with her charge, and Constance went back to the sick room to attend to her patient, while the Sister enjoyed a few hours' sleep.

One o'clock was Christabel's dinner-time, and Christabel's dinner was a business of no small importance in her mother's mind. One o'clock come, and there was no sign of Melanie and her charge, a curious thing, as Melanie was methodical and punctual to a praiseworthy degree, and was provided with a neat little silver watch to keep her acquainted with the time.

Two o'clock struck, and still no Melanie. Constance began to grow uneasy, and sent scouts to look for the nurse and child. But when three o'clock came and baby had not yet appeared, Constance became seriously alarmed, and put on her hat hastily, and went out to search for the missing nurse. She would not listen to the servants, who had just returned from their fruitless quest, and who begged her to let them go in fresh directions while she waited the result at home.

'No,' she said, 'I could not rest. I must go myself. Send to the police, any one, the proper authorities. Tell them my child is lost. Let them send in every direction. You have been to the ruins ?'

'Yes, ma'am.'

'And there was no one there ? You could hear nothing ?'

'No, ma'am,' answered Dawson the groom, 'the place was quite lonesome. There was nothing but grasshoppers chirruping.'

'The river !' thought Constance, white with horror. 'The ruins are only a little way from the river.'

She ran along the romantic pathway which followed the river bank for about half a mile, and then ascended the steep hill on the slope of which stood the battered old shell which had once been a feudal castle, with dungeons beneath its stately halls, and a deep and secret well for the safe putting away of troublesome enemies. Very peaceful looked the old ruins on this balmy September day, in the mellow afternoon sunshine, solitary, silent, deserted. There was no trace of nurse or child in the grassy court, or on the crumbling old rampart. Yes, just where the rampart looked down upon the river, just at that point where the short sunburnt grass sloped steepest, Constance Sinclair found a token of her child's presence, a toy dog, white, fleecy, and deliciously untrue to nature—an animal whose shapeless beauty and discordant yap had been the baby Christabel's delight.

Constance gave a little cry of joy.

'They have been here, they are somewhere near,' she thought, and then, suddenly, in the sweet summer stillness, the peril of this particular spot struck her—that steep descent—the sunburnt sward,

slippery as glass—the deep, swift current below;
the utter loneliness of the scene—no help at hand.

'Oh, God!' she cried. 'The river, the river!'

She looked round her with wild beseeching eyes,
as if she would have asked all nature to help her in
this great agony. There was no one within sight.
The nearest house was a cottage on the bank of the
river, about a hundred yards from the bottom of the
slope. A narrow footpath at the other end of the
rampart led to the bank, and by this path Constance
hurried down to make inquiries at the cottage.

The door was standing open, and there was a
noise of several voices within. Some one was lying
on a bed in a corner, and a group of peasant women
were round her ejaculating compassionately, 'Das
armes Mädchen. Ach, Himmel! Das ist schreck-
lich! Was gibt es?' and a good deal more of a
spasmodic and sympathetic nature.

A woman's garments, dripping wet, were hanging
in front of the stove, beside which sat an elderly
vinedresser with stolid countenance, smoking his
pipe.

Constance Sinclair put the women aside and

made her way to the bed.   It was Melanie who lay
there, wrapped in a blanket, sobbing hysterically.

'Melanie, where is my child?'

The girl shrieked and turned her face to the
wall.

'She risked her life to save it,' said the man in
German.   'The current is very rapid under the old
Schloss.   She plunged in after the baby.   I found
her in the water, clinging to the branch of a willow.
If I had been a little later she would have been
drowned.'

'And the child—my child?'

'Ach, mein Gott,' exclaimed the man, with a
shrug, 'no one has seen the poor child.   No one
knows.'

'My child is drowned!'

'Liebe Frau,' said one of the women, 'the
current is strong.   The little one was at play on
the rampart.   Its foot slipped, and it rolled down
the hill into the water.   This good girl ran down
after it, and jumped into the water.   My husband
found her there.   She tried to save the child, she
could do no more.   But the current was too strong·

Dear lady, be comforted. The good God will help you.'

' No, God is cruel,' cried Constance, ' I will never serve Him or believe in Him any more.'

And with this blasphemy, wrung from her tortured heart by the intolerable agony of that moment, a great wave of blood seemed to rush over Constance Sinclair's brain, and she fell senseless on the stone floor.

CHAPTER XI.

GETTING OVER IT.

BABY Christabel was drowned. Of that fact there could be no shadow of doubt in the minds of those who had loved her, although the sullen stream which had swallowed her lovely form refused to give it back. Perchance the Lurleys had taken her for their playfellow, and transformed her mortal beauty into something rich and strange.

The search for the dead was continued longer than such searches generally are; but the nets which dragged the river bed did not bring up the gold hair, or the sad drowned eyes that had once danced with joyous life. And if anything could add to Constance Sinclair's grief it was this last drop of bitter, the knowledge that her child would never rest in hallowed ground, that there was no quiet grave on which she might lay her aching head and feel nearer her darling, no spot of earth to which she

could press her lips and fancy she could be heard
by the little one lying in her pure shroud below,
asleep on Mother Earth's calm breast.

No, her little one was driven by winds and waves,
and had no resting-place under the weary stars.

Melanie Duport, when she recovered from the
horror of that one dreadful day, told her story
clearly enough. It was the same story she had
told the peasant woman whose husband rescued
her. Baby Christabel was playing on the rampart,
Melanie holding her securely, as she believed, when
the little one, attracted by the flight of a butterfly,
made a sudden spring—alas! Madame knew how
strong and active the dear angel was, and how difficult it was to hold her sometimes—and slipped out
of Melanie's arms on to the rampart, and from the
rampart—which was very low just there—as Madame
might have observed—on to the grass, and rolled
and rolled down to the river. It was all quick as
thought,—one moment, and that angel's white frock
was floating on the stream. Melanie tore down,
she knew not how; it was as if Heaven had given
her wings in that moment. The white frock was

still floating. Melanie plunged into the river! Ah, but what was her life at such a time? a nothing! Alas, she tried to grasp the frock, but the stream swept it from her; an instant, and one saw it no more. She felt herself sinking, and then her senses left her. She knew nothing till she woke in the cottage where Madame found her.

Melanie was a heroine in a small way after this sad event. The villagers thought her a wonderful young person. Her master rewarded her handsomely, and promised to retain her in his household till she should choose to marry. Her mistress was as grateful as despair can be for any benefit.

The light of Constance Sinclair's life had gone. Her one source of joy was turned to a fountain of bitterness. A dull and blank despair took possession of her. She did not succumb utterly to her grief. She struggled against it bravely, and she would accept no one's compassion or sympathy. One of her married sisters, a comfortable matron, with half a dozen healthy children in her nursery, offered to come and stay with Mrs. Sinclair, but this kindly offer was refused almost uncivilly.

'What good could you do me?' asked Constance. 'If you spoke to me of my darling I should hate you, yet I should always be thinking of her. Do you suppose you could comfort me by telling me about your herd of children, or by repeating little bits of Scripture, such as people quote in letters of condolence? No, there is no such thing as comfort for *my* grief. I like to sit alone and think of my pet, and be wretched in my own way. Don't be angry with me, dear, for writing so savagely. I sometimes feel as if I hated every one in the world, but happy mothers most of all.'

Gilbert Sinclair endured the loss of his little girl with a certain amount of philosophy. In the first place she was not a boy, and had offended him *ab initio* by that demerit. She had been a pretty little darling, no doubt, and he had had his moments of fondness for her; but his wife's idolatry of the child was an offence that had rankled deep. He had been jealous of his infant daughter. He put on mourning, and expressed himself deeply afflicted, but his burden did not press heavily. A boy would come, perhaps, by and by, and make amends for this present loss, and Constance would begin her baby-worship again.

Mr. Sinclair did not know that for some hearts there is no such thing as beginning again.

Martha Briggs recovered health and strength, but her grief for the lost baby was very genuine and unmistakable. Constance offered to keep her in her service, but this favour Martha declined with tears.

'No, ma'am, its best for both that we should part. I should remind you of——' (here a burst of sobs supplied the missing name), 'and you'd remind me. I'll go home. I'm more grateful than words can say for all your goodness; but oh! I hate myself so for being ill, and leaving my precious one to anybody else's care. I never, never shall forgive myself—never!'

So Martha went back to Davenant in her mistress's train, and there parted with her to return to the paternal roof, which was not very far off. It was not so with Melanie. She only clung to her mistress more devotedly after the loss of the baby.

If her dear lady would but let her remain with her as her own maid, she would be beyond measure happy. Was not hair-dressing the art in which she most delighted, and millinery the natural bent of her mind? Gilbert said the girl had acted nobly, and ought to be retained in his wife's service; so Constance, whose Abigail had lately left her to better herself by marriage with an aspiring butler, consented to keep Melanie as her personal attendant. She did this, believing with Gilbert that the girl deserved recompence; but Melanie's presence was full of painful associations, and kept the bitter memory of her lost child continually before her.

Constance went back to Davenant, and life flowed on in its slow and sullen course, somehow, without Baby Christabel. The two rooms that had been nurseries—two of the prettiest rooms in the big old house, one of them having French windows and a wide balcony, with a flight of steps leading down to a quaint old Dutch garden, shut in from the rest of the grounds by a holly hedge, now became temples dedicated to the lost. In these rooms Con-

stance spent all the time she could call her own.
But the business of life still went on, and there was
a great deal of time she could not call her own.
Gilbert, having dismissed the memory of his lost
child to the limbo of unpleasant recollections, resented his wife's brooding grief as a personal injury,
and was determined to give that sullen sorrow no indulgence.   When the hunting season was at its best,
and pheasant-shooting made one of the attractions of
Davenant, Mr. Sinclair determined to fill his house
with his own particular set—horsey men—men who
gave their minds to guns and dogs, and rarely opened
their mouths for speech except to relate some anec-
dote about an accomplished setter, or 'that liver-
coloured pointer of mine, you know;' or to dilate
upon the noble behaviour of 'that central fire Lan-
caster of mine,' in yesterday's battue; men who
devoted their nights to billiards, and whose conversation was of breaks and flukes, pockets and cannons.

'You'd better ask some women, Constance,' said
Gilbert, one Sunday morning in November, as they
sat at their *tête-à-tête* breakfast, the wife reading
her budget of letters, the husband with the *Field*

propped up in front of his coffee cup, and the *Sporting Gazette* at his elbow. 'I've got a lot of men coming next week, and you might feel yourself *de trop* in a masculine party.'

'Have you asked people, Gilbert? So soon!' said Constance, reproachfully.

'I don't know what you call soon. The pheasants are as wild as they can be, and Lord Highover's hounds have been out nearly a month. You'd better ask some nice young women; the right sort, you know, no nonsense about them.'

'I thought we should have spent this winter quietly, Gilbert,' said Constance, in a low voice, looking down at her black dress with its deep folds of crape, 'just this one winter.'

'That's sheer sentimentality,' exclaimed Gilbert, giving the *Field* an impatient twist as he folded it to get at his favourite column. 'What good would it do you or me to shut ourselves up in this dismal old house like a pair of superannuated owls? Would it bring back the poor little thing we've lost, or make her happier in paradise? No, Constance. She's happy. "Nothing can touch her more," as

Milton or somebody says. Egad, I think the poor
little darling is to be envied for having escaped all
the troubles and worries of life; for life at best is a
bad book, you can't hedge everything. Don't cry,
Constance. That long face of yours is enough to
send a fellow into an untimely grave. Let us get a
lot of pleasant people round us, and make the most
of this place while it's ours. We mayn't have it
always.'

This sinister remark fell upon an unheeding ear·
Constance Sinclair's thoughts had wandered far away
from that oak-panelled breakfast-room. They had
gone back to the sunny hill-side, the grassy rampart,
the swift and fatal river, the bright landscape which
had stamped itself upon her memory, indelibly, in
the one agonized moment in which she had divined
her darling's fate.

'Gilbert, I really am not fit to receive people,'
she said after a silence of some minutes, during
which Mr. Sinclair had amused himself by sundry
adventurous dips of his fork, like an old Jewish
priest's dive into the sacred seething-pot, into the
crockery case of a Perigord pie. 'If you have set

your heart upon having your friends this winter you had better let me go away, to Hastings or somewhere. It would be pleasanter for you to be free from the sight of my unhappiness.'

'Yes, and for you to find consolation elsewhere, no doubt. You would pretty soon find a consoler if I gave you your liberty.'

'Gilbert!'

'Oh, don't think to frighten me with your indignant looks. I have not forgotten the scene in this room when you heard of your old lover's supposed death. Sir Cyprian Davenant is 'in London, in high feather too, I understand ; for some ancient relation of his has been obliging enough to die and leave him another fortune. A pity you didn't wait a little longer, isn't it? A pity your father should have been in such a hurry to make his last matrimonial bargain.'

'Gilbert,' cried Constance, passionately, 'what have I ever done that you should dare to talk to me like this? How have I ever failed in my duty to you?'

'Shall I tell you? I won't say that, having

accepted me for your husband, you ought to have loved me. That would be asking too much. The ethics of the nineteenth century don't soar so high as that. But you might have pretended to care for me just a little. It would have been only civil, and it would have made the wheels of life go smoother for both of us.'

'I am not capable of pretending, Gilbert,' answered Constance, gravely. 'If you would only be a little more considerate, and give me credit for being what I am, your true and dutiful wife, I might give you as much affection as the most exacting husband could desire. I would, Gilbert,' she cried, in a voice choked by sobs, 'for the sake of our dead child.'

'Don't humbug,' said Gilbert, sulkily. 'We ought to understand each other by this time. As for running away from this house, or any other house of mine, to mope in solitude, or to find consolation among old friends, please comprehend that if you leave my house once you leave it for ever. I shall expect to see you at the head of my table. I shall expect you to surround yourself with pretty women.

I shall expect you to be a wife that a fellow may be proud of. Didn't I marry you to be a credit and an honour to me? I might have married as handsome a woman as you—one who understood me, and worshipped the ground I walked upon. But I wanted a wife whom all the world would admire.'

'I shall do my best to oblige you, Gilbert; but perhaps I might have been a better wife if you had let me take life my own way.'

From that time Constance Sinclair put aside all outward token of her grief. She wrote to the gayest and most pleasure-loving of her acquaintance— young married women, whose chief delight was to dress more expensively than their dearest friends, and to be seen at three parties on the same evening, and a few who were still spinsters, from no fault or foolishness of their own, since they had neglected neither pains nor art in the endeavour to secure an eligible partner for the dance of life. To these Constance wrote her letters of invitation, and the first sentence in each letter was sufficient to ensure an acceptance.

'DEAREST IDA,

'My husband is filling the house with men for the hunting season. Do come and save me from being bored to death by their sporting talk. Be sure you bring your hunting habit. Gilbert can give you a good mount,' &c., &c.

Whereupon dearest Ida, twisting about the little note, meditatively remarked to her last bosom friend and confidante, 'Odd that they should ask people so soon after the death of Mrs. Sinclair's baby,—drowned, too,—it was in all the papers. Davenant is a sweet house to stay at, quite liberty hall. Yes, I think I shall go, and if there are plenty of people I can finish out my ball dresses in the evenings.'

Before another Sunday came Davenant was full of people, the attics noisy with strange lady's-maids, the stables and harness-rooms full of life and bustle, not an empty stall or an unoccupied loose box in the long range of buildings, the billiard room and smoking room resonant with masculine laughter, unknown dogs pervading the out-buildings, and chained up in every available corner.

Constance Sinclair had put away her sombre

robes of crape and cashmere, and met her friends
with welcoming smiles, radiant in black silk and
lace, her graceful figure set off by the latest Parisian
fashion, which being the newest was of course considered infinitely the best.

'I thought she would have been in deeper
mourning,' said one of Mrs. Sinclair's dearest friends
to another during a confidential chat in a dusky
corner at afternoon tea.

'The men were so noisy with their haw-haw
talk, one could say what one liked,' remarked
Mrs. Millamount afterwards to Lady Loveall.

'Looks rather heartless, doesn't it?—an only
child, too. She might at least wear paramatta
instead of that black silk,—not even a mourning
silk. I suppose that black net trimmed with jet she
wore last night was from Worth. He is so fond of
smothering things with jet. It's one of his few
weaknesses.'

'My dear, you couldn't have looked at it
properly. Worth wouldn't have made her such a
thing if she had gone down on her knees to him.
The sleeve was positively antediluvian. Nice

house, isn't it ?—everything good style. What matches all these Clanyardes have made!'

'Is it true that she was engaged to Sir Cyprian Davenant ?'

'They say so. How sorry she must be! He has just come into quite a heap of money. Some old man down in the Lincolnshire fens left it him, quite a character, I believe. Never spent anything except on black-letter books, and those have been sold for a fortune at Sotheby's. Ah, Mr. Wyatt, how d'ye do ?' as the solicitor, newly arrived that afternoon, threaded his way towards the quiet corner, 'do come and sit here. You always know everything. Is it true that Sir Cyprian Davenant has come into a fortune ?'

'Nothing can be more true, unless it is that Mrs. Millamount looks younger and lovelier every season.'

'You horrid flatterer! You are worse than a French milliner. And is it true that Mrs. Sinclair and Sir Cyprian were engaged? But no, it would be hardly fair to ask you about that. You are a friend of the family.'

'As a friend of the family I am bound to inform

you that rumour is false on that point. There was
no engagement.'

' Really, now ?'

' But Sir Cyprian was madly in love with Miss
Clanyarde !'

' And she——'

'I was not in the lady's confidence; but I
believe that it was only my friend's poverty which
prevented their marriage.'

' How horribly mercenary!' cried Mrs. Millamount, who came of an ancient Irish family, proud as
Lucifer and poor as Lazarus, and who had been sacrificed in the blossom of her days—like Iphigenea, to
raise the wind—not to Diana, but to a rich stock-
broker. Perhaps, as the event had occurred a long
time ago, she may have forgotten how much more
Plutus had had to do with her marriage than Cupid.

CHAPTER XII.

CYPRIAN DAVENANT had inherited a fortune. Common rumour had not greatly exaggerated the amount of his wealth, though there was the usual disposition to expatiate upon the truth. Needy men looked at him with envy as he went in and out of his club, or sat in a quiet corner composedly reading the last Quarterly, or Edinburgh, and almost wondered that he was so well able to contain his spirits, and was not tempted to perform a savage dance of the Choctaw character, or to give expression to his rapture in a war-whoop.

'Hang it all, you know,' remarked an impecunious younger son, 'it aggravates a fellow to see Davenant take things so quietly. He doesn't even look cheerful. He doesn't invite the confidence of his necessitous friends. Such a knight of the rueful countenance would hardly stand a pony. And he won't play whist, or touch a billiard cue,—quite an unapproachable beast.'

A man cannot be lucky in all things. Sir Cyprian had set his life upon a cast, and the fortune of the game had been against him. The inheritance of this unexpected wealth seemed to him almost a purposeless and trivial stroke of fate. What could it avail him now? It could not give him Constance Clanyarde, or even restore the good old house in which his father and mother had lived and died. Time had set a gulf between him and happiness; and the fortune that came too late seemed rather the stroke of some mocking and ironical Fate than the gift of a benevolent destiny. He came back from Africa like a man who lives a charmed life, escaping all manner of perils, from the gripe of marsh fever to the jaws of crocodiles; while men who had valued existence a great deal more than he had done had succumbed and left their bones to bleach upon the sands of the Gold Coast, or to rot in a stagnant swamp. Cyprian Davenant had returned to find the girl he loved the wife of the man he most disliked. He heard of her marriage more in sorrow than in anger. He had not

expected to find her free. His knowledge of Lord
Clanyarde's character had assured him that his lordship's beautiful daughter would be made to marry
well. No fair Circassian, reared by admiring and
expectant relatives in the seclusion of her Caucasian
home, fattened upon milk and almonds to the stand-
ard of Oriental beauty, and in due course to be
carried to the slave market, had ever been brought
up with a more specific intention than that which
had ruled Lord Clanyarde in the education of his
daughters. They had all done well. He spent very
little time at Marchbrook now-a-days, but dawdled
away life agreeably, at his daughters' country houses
out of the season, at his clubs in the season, and felt
that his mission had been accomplished. No father
had ever done more for his children, and they had
cost him very little.

'What a comfort to have been blest with lovely
marriageable daughters, instead of lubberly sons>
squatting on a father's shoulders like the old man of
the mountain,' thought Lord Clanyarde, when he had
leisure to reflect upon his lot.

After that one visit in Park Lane, Sir Cyprian

Davenant had studiously avoided Mrs. Sinclair. He had very little inclination for society, and, although his friends were ready to make a fashionable lion of him upon the strength of his African explorations, he had strength of mind enough to refuse all manner of flattering invitations, and innumerable introductions to people who were dying to know him.

He took a set of chambers in one of the streets between the Strand and the river, surrounded himself with the books he loved, and set about writing the history of his travels. He had no desire to achieve fame by bookmaking, but a man must do something with his life. Sir Cyprian felt himself too old or too unambitious to enter one of the learned professions ; and he felt himself without motive for sustained industry. He had an income that sufficed for all his desires. He would write his book, tell the world the wonders he had seen, and then go back to Africa and see more wonders, and perhaps leave his bones along the road, as some of his fellow-travellers had done.

He heard of Constance Sinclair—heard of her as one of the lights in fashion's sidereal system—

holding her own against all competitors. He saw
her once or twice, between five and six on a June
afternoon, when the carriages were creeping slowly
along the Ladies' Mile, and the high-mettled horses
champing their bits and tugging at their bearing-
reins in that elegant martyrdom by which fashion
contrives to make the life of a three hundred
guinea pair of carriage horses a good deal worse
than that of a costmonger's donkey. He saw her
looking her loveliest, and concluded that she was
happy. She had all things that were reckoned
good in her world. Why should he suppose there
was anything wanting to her content ?

The lawyer's letter which told him of old Colonel
Gryffin's death, and the will which bequeathed to
him the bulk of the old man's fortune, found Sir
Cyprian in his quiet chambers near the river,
smoking the cigar of peace over the last new
treatise on metaphysics, by a German philosopher.
Lady Davenant had been a Miss Gryffin, and the
favourite niece of this ancient Anglo-Indian, Colonel
Gryffin, who had lived and died a bachelor. Sir
Cyprian had a faint recollection of seeing a testy

old gentleman, with a yellow complexion, at Davenant Park, in his nursery days, and having been told to call the old gentleman 'uncle,' whereupon he had revolted openly, and had declined to confer that honour upon such a wizened and tawny-complexioned atomy as the little old gentleman in question.

'My uncles are big,' he said. 'You're too little for an uncle.'

Soon afterwards the queer old figure had melted out of the home picture. Colonel Gryffin had gone back to the Lincolnshire fens, and his ancient missals and incunabula, and had lived so remote an existence that the chief feeling caused by his death was astonishment at the discovery that he had been so long alive.

Messrs. Dott and Gowunn, a respectable firm of family solicitors in Lincoln's Inn, begged to inform Sir Cyprian Davenant that his great-uncle on the maternal side, Colonel Gryffin, of Hobart Hall, near Hammerfield, Lincolnshire, had appointed him residuary legatee and sole executor to his will. Sir Cyprian was quite unmoved by the announce-

ment. Residuary legatee might mean a great deal,
or it might mean very little. He had a misty
recollection of being told that Colonel Gryffin was rich,
and was supposed to squander untold sums upon
Gutenberg Bibles, and other amiable eccentricities of
a bookish man. He had never been taught to expect
any inheritance from this ancient bachelor, and he had
supposed him for many years laid at rest under
the daisies of his parish churchyard.

The residuary legateeship turned out to mean
a very handsome fortune. The Colonel had not
spent a third of his income—despite his mania for
rare editions—and his money had been accumulat-
ing for the last thirty years. The missals and
Bibles, and antique Books of Hours, the Decameron,
and the fine old Shakespeare, were put up to auction
—by desire of the testator—and were sold for twice
and three times the sums the old Colonel had paid
for them. In a word, Sir Cyprian Davenant, who
had esteemed himself passing rich upon four hundred
a year, stood possessed of a hundred and twenty
thousand pounds.

It came too late to buy him the desire of his

heart, and, not being able to win for him this one blessing, it seemed almost useless.

James Wyatt was one of the first to congratulate Sir Cyprian upon this change of fortune.

'A pity the old gentleman did not die before you went to Africa,' he said, sympathetically. 'It would have squared things for you and Miss Clanyarde.'

'Miss Clanyarde made a very good marriage,' answered Cyprian, too proud to bare his old wound even to friendly James Wyatt. 'She is happy.'

Mr. Wyatt shrugged his shoulders dubiously.

'Who knows?' he said. 'We see our friends' lives from the outside, and, like a show at a fair, the outside is always the best part of the performance.'

This happened while Mr. and Mrs. Sinclair were at Schönesthal. Soon came the tidings of Baby Christabel's fate, briefly told in a newspaper paragraph, and Cyprian Davenant's heart bled for the woman he had once loved. He was not a little surprised when James Wyatt called upon him one day in November and told him he was going

down to Davenant, where there was to be a house
full of company.

'So soon after the little girl's death!' exclaimed
Sir Cyprian.

'Yes, it is rather soon, no doubt.   But they
would be moped to death   at Davenant without
people.   Sackcloth and ashes are quite out of
fashion, you see.   People don't go in for intense
mourning now-a-days.'

'People have hearts, I suppose, even in the
nineteenth century?' said Sir Cyprian, somewhat
bitterly.   'I should have thought Mrs. Sinclair
would have felt the loss of her little girl very
deeply.'

'We don't know what *she* may feel,' returned
Wyatt.   'Gilbert likes his own way.'

'You don't mean to say that he ill-uses his wife?'
asked Sir Cyprian, alarmed.

'Ill-usage is a big word.   We don't employ it now-
a-days,' replied Mr. Wyatt, with his imperturbable
smile. 'Gilbert Sinclair is my client, and an excellent
one, as you know. It would ill become me to disparage
him; but I must admit that he and Mrs. Sinclair

are not the happiest couple whose domestic hearth
I have ever sat by. She had some secret grief, even
before the death of her child, and made up for being
very brilliant in society by being exceedingly dull at
home. I don't expect to find her very lively now
that she has lost the only being she really cared for.
She absolutely worshipped that child.'

This conversation gave Sir Cyprian Davenant
material for much sad thought. To know that
Constance was unhappy seemed to bring her nearer
to him. It brought back the thought of the old days
when those innocent eyes had looked into his,
eloquent with unconscious love, when Constance
Clanyarde had given him her heart without thought
for to-morrow, happy in the knowledge that she was
loved, believing her lover strong to conquer Fate and
Fortune. And he had brought the chilly light of
worldly wisdom to bear on this dream of Arcady.
He had been strong, self-denying, and had renounced
his own happiness in the hope of securing hers.
And now Fate laughed him to scorn with this gift of
vain riches; and he found that his worldly wisdom
had been supreme folly.

'What a self-sufficient fool, what an idiot I have been!' he said to himself in an agony of remorse. 'And now what atonement can I make to her for my folly? Can I defend her from the purse-proud snob she has been sold to? can I save her wounded heart one pang? can I be near her in her hour of misery, or offer one drop of comfort from a soul overflowing with tenderness and pity? No, to approach her is to do her a wrong. But I can watch at a distance, perhaps. I may use other eyes. My money may be of some use in buying her faithful service from others. God bless her! I consecrate my days to her service: distant or near, I will be her friend and her defender!'

Two days later Sir Cyprian met Lord Clanyarde at that nobleman's favourite club. It was a club which Cyprian Davenant rarely used, although he had been a member ever since his majority, and it may be that he went out of his beaten track in the hope of encountering Constance Sinclair's father.

Lord Clanyarde was very cordial and complimentary upon his friend's altered fortunes.

'You must feel sorry for having parted with

Davenant,' he said, ' when you might so easily have
kept it.'

'Davenant is rather too big for a confirmed
bachelor.'

' True. It would have been a white elephant, I
dare say. Sinclair has improved the place considerably. You ought to come down and have a look
at it. I'm going to Marchbrook to shoot next week.
Come and stay with me,' added Lord Clanyarde with
heartiness, not at all prepared to be taken at his
word.

'I shall be charmed,' said Sir Cyprian, to his
lordship's infinite astonishment.

People generally took his invitations for what
they were worth, and declined them. But here was
a man fresh from the centre of Africa, who hardly
understood the language of polite society.

CHAPTER XIII.

ALL went merrily at Davenant during the brief bleak days of November and December, though the master of the house was not without his burden of secret cark and care. That magnificent iron and coal producing estate in the north had not been yielding quite so much hard cash lately as its owner expected from it. Strikes and trade-unionism had told upon Mr. Sinclair's income. The coal market had fluctuated awkwardly. Belgium had been tapping the demand for iron. There was plenty of money coming in, of course, from Gilbert's large possessions; but unfortunately there was also a great deal going out. The Newmarket stables had cost a small fortune; the Newmarket horses had been unlucky; and Gilbert's book for the last three or four seasons had been a decided failure.

'The fact is, Wyatt,' he remarked to that confidential adviser one dull afternoon over a *tête-à-tête* game at billiards, 'I'm spending too much money.'

'Have you only just found that out?' asked the solicitor, with a calm sneer.

'The purchase of this confounded place took too much of my capital, and these strikes and lock-outs coming on the top of it——'

'Not to mention your vicious habit of plunging,' remarked Mr. Wyatt, parenthetically, taking a careful aim at the distant red.

'Have very nearly stumped me.'

'Why not sell Davenant? You don't want such a big barrack of a place, and—Mrs. Sinclair isn't happy here.'

'No,' said Gilbert, with a smothered oath, 'the associations are too tender.'

'I could get you a purchaser to-morrow.'

'Yes, at a dead loss, no doubt. You fellows live by buying and selling, and you don't care how much your client loses by a transaction that brings grist to your mill.'

'I can get you the money you gave for Davenant, timber and all.'

'Who's your purchaser?'

'I'd rather not mention his name yet awhile.   He
is a quiet party, and wouldn't like to be talked about.'

'I understand.   Some city cad, who has made his
money in the zoological line.'

'How zoological?'

'Bulling and bearing.   Well, if those beastly
colliers hold out much longer, he may have Davenant
and welcome.   But he must take my new furniture
at a valuation.   I've paid no end of money for it.'

'What did you do with the Jacobean oak?'

'Oh, the old sticks are put away somewhere, I
believe, in lofts and lumber-rooms, and servants' bed-
rooms.'

Some of Mr. Sinclair's other guests dropped into
the billiard-room at this juncture, and there was no
more said about the sale of Davenant.

Nobody—not even his worst enemy, and no doubt
among his numerous friends he had several foes—
could deny Mr. Wyatt's merits as a guest in a
country house.   He was just the kind of man to keep
things going—a past master in all social accomplish-
ments,—and Gilbert Sinclair graciously allowed him

to take the burden of amusing everybody upon his
shoulders, while the master of the house went his own
way, and hunted or shot at his own pleasure. Mr.
Sinclair liked to fill his house with people, but he
had no idea of sacrificing his own inclination to their
entertainment ; he thought he did quite enough for
them in giving them what he elegantly called ' the
run of their teeth,' and the free use of his second-rate
hunters.

On Mr. Wyatt, therefore, devolved the duty of
keeping things going—devising the day's amusements, protecting the ladies of the party from the
selfishness of neglectful and unappreciative mankind,
arranging picnic luncheons in keepers' lodges, at
which the fair sex might assist—finding safe mounts
for those aspiring damsels who wanted to ride to
hounds—planning private theatricals, and stimu-
lating the musical members of the society to the
performance of part-songs in a business-like and
creditable manner.

He had done all these things last winter, and the
winter before, but on those occasions he had been
aided in his task. Constance Sinclair had given him

her hearty co-operation. She had played her part of
hostess with grace and spirit—had allowed no cloud
of thought or memory to obscure the brightness of
the present moment. She had given herself up, heart
and soul, to the duties of her position, and her
friends had believed her to be the happiest of women,
as well as the most fortunate. To seem thus had
cost her many an effort; but she had deemed this
one of her obligations as Gilbert Sinclair's wife.

Now all was changed. Her husband had been
obeyed, but that obedience was all which Constance
Sinclair's sense of duty could now compel. She sat
like a beautiful statue at the head of her husband's
table, she moved about among her guests with as
little part in their pleasures and amusements as if
she had been a picture on the wall—courteous
to all, but familiar with none. She seemed to
live apart from her surroundings—a strange and
silent life, whose veil of shadow even sympathy
failed to penetrate. Mrs. Millamount, not unfriendly,
despite her frivolity, had tried to get Constance to
talk of her bereavement, but the wounded heart was
galled by the gentlest touch.

'It's very kind of you,' she said, divining her friend's motive, 'but I'd rather not talk of her. Nothing can ever lessen my grief, and I like best to keep it quite to myself.'

'How you must hate us all for being here!' said Mrs. Millamount, moved with compunction at the incongruity between that house full of company and the mother's desolate heart. 'It seems quite abominable for us to be thinking of nothing but pleasure while you bear your burden alone.'

'Nobody could divide it with me, or make it lighter for me,' answered Constance, gently. 'Pray do not trouble yourself about my sorrows. If I could hide them better I would. Gilbert likes to be surrounded with pleasant faces, and I am very glad that he should be pleased.'

'She's quite too good to live,' remarked the sprightly Mrs. Millamount to her friend Lady Loveall that evening. 'But do you know I'm afraid there's something a little wrong here,' and Flora Millamount touched her ivory forehead suggestively with the tip of her Watteau fan.

James Wyatt was not a sportsman. He was an

excellent judge of a horse, rode well, and knew as much about guns as the men who were continually handling them, but he neither shot nor hunted, and he had never been known to speculate upon the turf. These things were for his clients—a very pretty way of running through handsome fortunes and bringing their owner to the Jews—not for him. He could take his amusement out of other men's follies and remain wise himself. Life to him was an agreeable and instructive spectacle, which he assisted at as comfortably as he heard 'Don Giovanni' from his stall in the middle of the third row ; and when the foul fiend of insolvency whisked off one of his dearest friends to the infernal regions where bankrupts and outlaws inhabit, he felt what a nice thing it was to be only a spectator of the great drama.

Not being a sportsman, Mr. Wyatt had a good deal of time to himself at Davenant despite his general usefulness. There were rainy mornings when the men were out shooting, and the 'bus had not yet started for the point of rendezvous with the ladies and the luncheon. These leisure hours Mr. Wyatt improved by strolling about the corridors,

looking at the old pictures—for the most part in that
meditative mood in which a man sees very little of
the picture he seems to contemplate—and occasionally
varying his meditations by a quiet flirtation with
Melanie Duport.   That young person had plenty of
leisure for perambulating the corridors between
breakfast and dinner.   Mrs. Sinclair was by no means
an exacting mistress, and Melanie's life at Davenant
was one of comparative idleness.   Her superiority of
mind showed itself in a calm contempt for her fellow-
servants, and she was rarely to be found in the
servants' rooms.   She preferred the retirement of
her own bedchamber, and a French novel lent her
by that good-natured Mr. Wyatt, who had always a
supply of the newest and worst Parisian literature
in his portmanteau.   On this dull December morning—a day of gray clouds and frequent showers
—Mr. Wyatt stood before a doubtful Vandyke,
smoking meditatively, and apparently absorbed in
a critical examination of Prince Rupert's slouched
beaver and ostrich plume, when Melanie's light
quick step at the other end of the gallery caught
his ear.

He turned slowly round to meet her, puffing lazily at his cigar.

'Eh, la belle,' he exclaimed, 'even an English December does not dim the lustre of those Southern eyes.'

'I was born in the *Quartier Latin*, and my parents were all that there is of the most Parisian,' answered Melanie, scornfully.

'Then you must have stolen those eyes of yours from one of the Murillos in the Louvre. What news, little one?'

'Only that I find myself more and more weary of this dismal old barrack.'

'Come, now, Melanie, you must confess you have a good time of it here.'

'Oh, as for that, perhaps I ought not to complain. My mistress is very gentle, too gentle ; it gnaws me to the heart to see her silent grief. That preys upon my mind.'

Here Melanie squeezed out a tear, which she removed from her pearl-powdered cheek—a very sallow cheek under the powder—daintily, with the corner of a hem-stitched handkerchief.

'You are too compassionate, little one,' said Mr. Wyatt, putting his arm round her waist consolingly. Perhaps he had gone a little too far with these leisure half-hours of flirtation. He had an idea that the girl was going to be troublesome. Tears augured mischief.

'*C'est dommage*,' murmured Melanie, 'I have the heart too tender.'

'Don't fret, my angel. See here, pretty one, I have brought you another novel,' taking a paper-covered book from his pocket.

'Belot ?'

'No, Zola.'

'I don't want it. I won't read it. Your novels are full of lies. They describe men who will make any sacrifice for the woman they love—men who will take a peasant girl from her hovel, or a grisette from her garret, and make her a queen. There are no such men. I don't believe in them,' cried the girl, passionately, her eyes flashing fire.

'Don't be angry, Melanie. Novels would be dull if they told only the truth.'

'They would be very amusing if they described men of your pattern,' retorted Melanie. 'Men who

say sweet things without meaning them—who flatter
every woman they talk to, who turn a foolish girl's
head with their pretty speeches and caressing ways,
and then laugh at her folly. Yes, as you are laughing
at me,' cried Melanie, exasperated by Mr. Wyatt's
placid smile.

'No, my sweet, I am only admiring you,' he
replied, calmly. 'What have I done to raise this
tempest ? '

'What have you done?' cried Melanie, and then
burst into tears, real tears this time, which seriously
damaged the pearl powder. 'I am sure I don't
know why I should care so much for you. You are
not handsome. You are not even young.'

'Perhaps not, but I am very agreeable,' said James
Wyatt, complacently. 'Don't cry, *ma belle*, only be
patient and reasonable, and perhaps I shall be able
to prove to you some day that there are men, real
living men, who are capable of any sacrifice for the
woman they love.'

Melanie allowed herself to be appeased by this
rather vague speech, but she was only half
convinced.

'Tell me only one thing,' she said. 'Who is that lady I saw at Schönesthal? and why were you so anxious to please her?'

James Wyatt's smooth face clouded at this question.

"She is related to me, and I knew she had been badly used. Hush, my dear! walls have ears. There are things we mustn't talk about here.'

'What is the lady's real name?'

'Madame Chose.   She comes of the oldest branch of the family, altogether *grande dame*, I assure you.'

'I wish she would take me into her service.'

'Why, you are better off here than with her.'

'I don't think so. I should see more of you if I lived with that lady.'

'There you are wrong. I see Madame Chose very rarely.'

'I don't believe you.'

'Melanie, that's extremely rude.'

'I believe that you are passionately in love with that lady, and that is why——'

'Not another word,' exclaimed James Wyatt, 'there's the luncheon-bell, and I must be off. You'd

better take Zola.   You'll find him more amusing
than the talk in the servants' hall.'

Melanie took the volume sullenly, and walked
away without a word.

'What a little spitfire!' mused Mr. Wyatt, as he
went slowly down the wide oak staircase. 'She
has taken my pretty speeches seriously, and means
to make herself obnoxious.   This comes of putting
one's self in the power of the inferior sex. If I had
trusted a man, as I trusted that girl, it would have
been a simple matter of business.   He would have
been extortionate, perhaps, and there an end. But
Mademoiselle Duport makes it an affair of the
heart, and I dare say will worry my life out before
I have done with her.'

CHAPTER XIV.

SIR CYPRIAN DAVENANT had not forgotten that dinner at Richmond given by Gilbert Sinclair a little while before his departure for Africa, at which he had met the handsome widow to whom Mr. Sinclair was then supposed to be engaged. The fact was brought more vividly back to his mind by a circumstance that came under his notice the evening after he had accepted Lord Clanyarde's invitation to Marchbrook.

He had been dining at his club with an old college friend, and had consented, somewhat unwillingly, to an adjournment to one of the theatres near the Strand, at which a popular burlesque was being played for the three hundred and sixty-fifth time. Sir Cyprian entertained a cordial detestation of this kind of entertainment, in which the low comedian of the company enacts a distressed damsel in short petticoats and a flaxen wig, while pretty actresses swagger in costumes of the cavalier period, and ape the manners of the music-hall swell. But it was ten o'clock. The friends had recalled all the old Oxford follies in the days when they were undergraduates together in Tom Quad. They had exhausted these reminiscences and a magnum of Lafitte, and though Sir Cyprian would have gladly gone back to his chambers and his books, Jack Dunster, his friend, was of a livelier temperament, and wanted to finish the evening.

'Let's go and see "Hercules and Omphale" at the Kaleidoscope,' he said. 'It's no end of fun. Jeemson plays Omphale in a red wig, and Minnie Vavasour looks awfully fascinating in pink satin boots and a lion-skin. We shall be just in time for the break-down.'

Sir Cyprian assented with a yawn. He had seen fifty such burlesques as 'Hercules and Omphale,' in the days when such things had their charm for him too, when he could be pleased with a pretty girl in pink satin Hessians, or be moved to laughter by Jeemson's painted nose and falsetto scream.

They took a hansom and drove to the Kaleidoscope, a bandbox of a theatre screwed into an awkward corner of one of the narrowest streets in London—a street at which well-bred carriage horses accustomed to the broad thoroughfares of Belgravia shied furiously.

It was December, and there was no one worth speaking of in town ; but the little Kaleidoscope was crowded notwithstanding. There were just a brace of empty stalls in a draughty corner for Sir Cyprian and Mr. Dunster.

The breakdown was on, the pretty little Hercules flourishing his club, and exhibiting a white round arm with a diamond bracelet above the elbow. Omphale was showing her ankles to the delight of the groundlings, the violins were racing one another, and the flute squeaking its shrillest in a vulgar nigger melody, accentuated by rhythmical bangs on the big drum. The audience was in raptures, and rewarded the exertions of band and dancers with a double recall. Sir Cyprian stifled another yawn and looked round the house.

Among the vacuous countenances all intent on the

spectacle, there was one face which was out of the
common, and which expressed a supreme weariness.
A lady was sitting alone in a stage box, with one
rounded arm resting indolently on the velvet cushion
—an arm that might have been carved in marble, bare
to the elbow, its warm human ivory relieved by the
yellow hue of an old Spanish point ruffle.   Where
had Cyprian Davenant seen that face before ?

The lady had passed the first bloom of youth
but her beauty was of the character that does not
fade with youth.   She was of the Pauline Borghese
type, a woman worthy to be modelled by a new
Canova.

'I remember,' said Sir Cyprian to himself. 'It
was at that Richmond dinner I met her.   She is
the lady Gilbert Sinclair was to have married.'

He felt a curious interest in this woman whose
name even he had forgotten.   Why had not Sinclair
married her?   She was strikingly handsome, with a
bolder, grander beauty than Constance Clanyarde's
fragile and poetic loveliness—a woman whom such a
man as Sinclair might have naturally chosen.   Just
as such a man would choose a high-stepping chestnut

horse, without being too nice as to fineness and delicacy of line.

'And I think from the little I saw that the lady was attached to him,' mused Sir Cyprian.

He glanced at the stage box several times before the end of the performance. The lady was quite alone, and sat in the same attitude, fanning herself languidly, and hardly looking at the stage. Just as the curtain fell, Sir Cyprian heard the click of the box door, and looking up saw that a gentleman had entered. The lady rose, and the gentleman came a little forward to assist in the arrangement of her ermine-lined mantle.

It was Gilbert Sinclair.

'What did you think of it?' asked Jack Dunster as they went out into the windy lobby where people were crowded together waiting for their carriages.

'Abominable,' murmured Sir Cyprian.

'Why, Minnie Vavasour is the prettiest actress in London, and Jeemson's almost equal to Toole.'

'I beg your pardon. I was not thinking of the burlesque,' answered Sir Cyprian, hastily.

Gilbert and his companion were just in front
of them.

'Shall I go and look for your carriage?' asked
Mr. Sinclair.

'If you like,' answered the lady. 'But as you
left me to sit out this dreary rubbish by myself all
the evening, you might just as well have let me
find my way to my carriage.'

'Don't be angry with me for breaking my
engagement. I was obliged to go out shooting with
some fellows, and I didn't leave Maidstone till nine
o'clock. I think I paid you a considerable compliment in travelling thirty miles to hand you to your
carriage. No other woman could exact so much
from me.'

'You are not going back to Davenant to-night?'

'No, there is a supper on at the Albion. Lord
Colsterdale's trainer is to be there, and I expect
to get a wrinkle or two from him. A simple matter
of business, I assure you.'

'Mrs. Walsingham's carriage,' roared the water-
man.

'Mrs. Walsingham,' thought Sir Cyprian, who

was squeezed into a corner with his friend, walled up by opera-cloaked shoulders, and within ear-shot of Mr. Sinclair. 'Yes, that's her name.'

'That saves you all trouble,' said Mrs. Walsingham. 'Can I set you down anywhere?'

'No, thanks; the Albion's close by.'

Sir Cyprian struggled out of his corner just in time to see Gilbert shut the brougham door and walk off through the December drizzle.

'So that acquaintance is not a dropped one,' he thought. 'It augurs ill for Constance.'

Three days later he was riding out Barnet way, in a quiet country lane, as rural and remote in aspect as an accommodation road in the shires, when he passed a brougham with a lady in it—Mrs. Walsingham again, and again alone.

'This looks like fatality,' he thought.

He had been riding Londonwards, but turned his horse and followed the carriage. This solitary drive, on a dull, gray winter day, so far from London, struck him as curious. There might be nothing really suspicious in the fact. Mrs. Walsingham might have friends in this northern district. But

after what he had seen at the Kaleidoscope, Sir
Cyprian was inclined to suspect Mrs. Walsingham.
That she still cared for Sinclair he was assured. He
had seen her face light up when Gilbert entered the
box—he had seen that suppressed anger which is
the surest sign of a jealous, exacting love. Whether
Gilbert still cared for her was an open question. His
meeting her at the theatre might have been a
concession to a dangerous woman rather than a
spontaneous act of devotion.

Sir Cyprian followed the brougham into the
sequestered village of Totteridge, where it drew up
before the garden gate of a neat cottage, with green
blinds, and a half-glass door; a cottage which looked
like the abode of a spinster annuitant.

Here Mrs. Walsingham alighted and went in,
opening the half-glass door with the air of a person
accustomed to enter.

He rode a little way further, and then walked his
horse gently back. The brougham was still standing before the garden gate, and Mrs. Walsingham
was walking up and down a gravel path by the
side of the house with a woman and a child, a

child in a scarlet hood, just able to toddle along the path, sustained on each side by a supporting hand.

'Some poor relation's child, perhaps,' thought Cyprian. 'A friendly visit on the lady's part.'

He had ridden further than he intended, and stopped at the little inn to give his horse a feed of corn and an hour's rest, while he strolled through the village and looked at the old-fashioned church-yard. The retired spot was not without its interest. Yonder was Coppet Hall, the place Lord Melbourne once occupied, and which at a later period passed into the possession of the author of that splendid series of novels which reflect, as in a magic mirror, all the varieties of life from the age of Pliny to the eve of the Franco-Prussian war.

'Who lives in that small house with the green blinds?' asked Sir Cyprian of the ostler, as he mounted his horse to ride home.

'It's been took furnished, sir, by a lady from London, for her nurse and baby.'

'Do you know the lady's name?'

'I can't say that I do, sir. They has their beer

from the brewer, and pays ready money for every-think. But I see the lady's brougham go by not above half an hour ago.'

'Curious,' thought Sir Cyprian. 'Mrs. Walsingham is not rising in my opinion.'

CHAPTER XV.

IN accepting Lord Clanyarde's invitation Cyprian
Davenant had but one thought, one motive.   He
wanted to be near Constance.   Not to see her.
Dear as she still was to him, he had no desire to see
her.   He knew that such a meeting could bring with
it only bitterness for both.   But he wanted to be
near her, to ascertain, at once and for ever, the
whole unvarnished truth as to her domestic life, the
extent of her unhappiness, if she was unhappy.
Rumour might exaggerate.   Even the practical solicitor, James Wyatt, might. represent the state of
affairs as worse than it was.   The human mind leans
to vivid colouring, and bold dramatic effect.   An
ill-used wife and a tyrannical husband present one of
those powerful pictures which society contemplates
with interest.   Society—represented generally by Lord
Dundreary—likes to pity, just as it likes to wonder.

At Marchbrook, Sir Cyprian was likely to learn the truth, and to Marchbrook he went, affecting an interest in pheasants, and in Lord Clanyarde's conversation, which was like a rambling and unrevised edition of the Greville Memoirs, varied with turf reminiscences.

There was wonderfully fine weather in that second week of December; clear autumnal days, blue skies and sunny mornings. The pheasants were shy, and after the first day Sir Cyprian left them to their retirement, preferring long lonely rides among the scenes of his boyhood, and half-hours of friendly chat with ancient gaffers and goodies who remembered his father and mother, and the days when Davenant had still held up its head in the occupation of the old race.

'This noo gentleman, he do spend a power o' money; but he'll never be looked up to like old Sir Cyprian,' said a gray-headed village sage, leaning over his gate to talk to young Sir Cyprian.

In one of his rounds Cyprian Davenant looked in upon the abode of Martha Briggs, who was still at home.

Her parents were in decent circumstances, and not eager to see their daughter 'suited' with a new service.

Martha remembered Sir Cyprian as a friend of Mrs. Sinclair's before her marriage. She had seen them out walking together in the days when Constance Clanyarde was still in the nursery: for Lord Clanyarde's youngest daughter had known no middle stage between the nursery and her Majesty's drawing-room. Indeed, Martha had had her own ideas about Sir Cyprian, and had quite made up her mind that Miss Constance would marry him.

She was therefore disposed to be confidential, and with very slight encouragement told Cyprian all about that sad time at Schönesthal, how her mistress had nursed her through the scarlet fever, and how the sweetest child that ever lived had been drowned, owing to that horrid French girl's carelessness.

'It's all very well to boast of jumping into the river to save the darling,' exclaimed Martha, 'but why did she go and take the precious pet into a dangerous place? When I had her I could see danger beforehand. I didn't want to be told that a hill was steep, or that grass was slippery. I never did like foreigners, and now I hate them like poison,' cried Miss Briggs, as if under the impression that the whole continent of Europe was implicated in Baby Christabel's death.

'It must have been a great grief to Mrs. Sinclair,' said Sir Cyprian.

'Ah, poor dear, she'll never hold up her head again,' sighed Martha. 'I saw her in church last Sunday, in the beautifullest black bonnet, and if ever I saw any one going to heaven it's her. And Mr. Sinclair will have a lot of company, and there are all the windows at Davenant blazing with light till past twelve o'clock every night—my cousin James is a pointsman on the South-Eastern, and sees the house from the line—while that poor sweet lady is breaking her heart.'

'But surely Mr. Sinclair would defer to his wife in these things?' suggested Sir Cyprian.

'Not he, sir. For the last twelve months that I was with my dear lady I seldom heard him say a kind word to her. Always snarling and sneering. I do believe he was jealous of that precious innocent

because Mrs. Sinclair was so fond of her. I'm sure
if it hadn't been 'for that dear baby my mistress
would have been a miserable woman.'

This was a bad hearing, and Sir Cyprian went
back to Marchbrook that evening sorely depressed.

He had declined to visit Davenant with Lord
Clanyarde, owning frankly that there was no friendly
feeling between Gilbert Sinclair and himself. Lord
Clanyarde perfectly understood the state of the case,
but affected to be supremely ignorant. He was a
gentleman whose philosophy was to take things easy.
Not to disturb Camerina, or any other social lake
beneath whose tranquil water there might lurk a
foul and muddy bottom, was a principle with Lord
Clanyarde. But the nobleman, though philosophic
and easy tempered, was not without a heart. There
was a strain of humanity in the sybarite and world-
ling, and when, at a great dinner at Davenant, he
saw the impress of a broken heart upon the statu-
esque beauty of his daughter's face, he was touched
with pity and alarm. To sell his daughter to the
highest bidder had not seemed to him in any wise a
crime; but he would not have sold her to age or

deformity, or to a man of notoriously evil life. Gilbert Sinclair had appeared to him a very fair sample of the average young Englishman. Not stainless, perhaps. Lord Clanyarde did not inquire too closely into details. The suitor was good-looking, good-natured, open-handed, and rich. What more could any dowerless young woman require?

Thus had Lord Clanyarde reasoned with himself when he hurried on his youngest daughter's marriage; and, having secured for her this handsome establishment, he had given himself no further concern about her destiny. No daughter of the house of Clanyarde had ever appeared in the divorce court. Constance was a girl of high principles—always went to church on saints' days, abstained in Lent, and would be sure to go on all right.

But at Davenant, on this particular evening, Lord Clanyarde saw a change in his daughter that chilled his heart. He talked to her, and she answered him absently, with the air of one who only half understands. Surely this argued something more than grief for her dead child.

He spoke to Gilbert Sinclair, and gave frank utterance to his alarm.

'Yes, she is very low-spirited,' answered Gilbert, carelessly, 'still fretting for the little girl. I thought it would cheer her to have people about her—prevent her dwelling too much upon that unfortunate event. But I really think she gets worse. It's rather hard upon me. I didn't marry to be miserable.'

'Have you had a medical opinion about her?' asked Lord Clanyarde, anxiously.

'Oh, yes, she has her own doctor. The little old man who used to attend her at Marchbrook. She prefers him to any other doctor, and he knows her constitution, no doubt. He prescribes tonics, and so on, and recommends change of scene by and by, when she gets a little stronger; but my own opinion is that if she would only make an effort, and not brood upon the past, she'd soon get round again. Oh, by the way, I hear you have Sir Cyprian Davenant staying with you.'

'Yes, he has come down to shoot some of my pheasants.'

'I didn't know you and he were so thick.'

'I have known him ever since he was a boy, and knew his father before him.'

'I wonder, as your estates joined, you did not knock up a match between him and Constance.'

'That wouldn't have been much good, as he couldn't keep his estate.'

'No. It's a pity that old man in Lincoln-shire didn't take it into his head to die a little sooner.'

'I find no fault with destiny for giving me you as a son-in-law, and I hope you are not tired of the position,' said Lord Clanyarde, with a look that showed Gilbert he must pursue his insinuations no further.

Lord Clanyarde went home and told Sir Cyprian what he had seen, and his fears about Constance. He reproached himself bitterly for his share in bringing about the marriage, being all the more induced to regret that act now that change of fortune had made Cyprian Davenant almost as good a match as Gilbert Sinclair.

'How short-sighted we mortals are!' thought the

anxious father. 'I did not even know that Cyprian had a rich bachelor uncle.'

Sir Cyprian heard Lord Clanyarde's account in grave silence.

'What do you mean to do?' he asked.

'What can I do? Poor child, she is alone, and must bear her burden unaided. I cannot come between her and her husband. It would take very little to make me quarrel with Sinclair, and then where should we be? If she had a mother living it would be different.'

'She has sisters,' suggested Cyprian.

'Yes, women who are absorbed by the care of their own families, and who would not go very far out of their way to help her. With pragmatical husbands, too, who would make no end of mischief if they were allowed to interfere. No, we must not make a family row of the business. After all, there is no specific ground for complaint. She does not complain, poor child. I'll go to Davenant early to-morrow and see her alone. Perhaps I can persuade her to be frank with me.'

'You might see the doctor, and hear his account of her,' said Cyprian.

'Yes, by the way, little Dr. Webb, who attended my girls from their cradles.   An excellent little man. I'll send for him to-morrow and consult him about my rheumatism.   He must know a good deal about my poor child.'

Lord Clanyarde was with his daughter soon after breakfast next morning.   He found her in that pretty old-fashioned apartment called the balcony room, which had been Christabel's day nursery, and which had a door of communication with Mrs. Sinclair's dressing-room.   It was the end of the north wing, and was overlooked by the window of Gilbert's study—study *par excellence*—but dressing room and gunnery in fact.

Constance received her father with affection, but he could not win her confidence.   It might be that she had nothing to confide.   She made no complaint against her husband.

'Why do I find you sitting here alone, Constance, while the house is full of cheerful people?' asked Lord Clanyarde.   'I heard the billiard balls going as I came through the hall, early as it is.'

'Gilbert likes company and I do not,' answered Constance, quietly. 'We each take our own way.'

'That does not sound like a happy union, pet,' said her father.

'Did you expect me to be happy—with Gilbert Sinclair?'

'Yes, my love, or I would never have asked you to marry him. No, Constance. Of course it was an understood thing with me that you must marry well, as your sisters had done before you; but I meant you to marry a man who would make you happy; and if I find that Sinclair ill-uses you, or slights you, egad, he shall have no easy reckoning with me.'

'My dear father, pray be calm. He is very good to me. I have never complained—I never shall complain. I try to do my duty, for I know that I have done him a wrong, for which a life of duty and obedience can hardly atone.'

'Wronged him, child! How have you wronged him?'

'By marrying him when my heart was given to another.'

'Nonsense, pet; a mere school-girl penchant. If that kind of thing were to count, there's hardly a wife living who has not wronged her husband. Every romantic girl begins by falling in love with a detrimental; but the memory of that juvenile attachment has no more influence on her married life than the recollection of her favourite doll. You must get such silly notions out of your head. And you should try to be a little more lively, and join in Sinclair's amusements. No man likes a gloomy wife. And remember, love, the past is past—no tears can bring back our losses. If they could, hope would prevent our crying, as somebody judiciously observes.'

Constance sighed and was silent, whereupon Lord Clanyarde embraced his daughter tenderly and departed, feeling that he had done his duty. She was much depressed, poor child, but no doubt time would set things right; and as to Sinclair's maltreating her, that was out of the question. No man above the working-classes ill-uses his wife now-a-days. Lord Clanyarde made quite light of his daughter's troubles when he met Sir Cyprian at lunch. Sinclair was a good fellow enough at bottom, he assured Sir Cyprian; a little too fond of pleasure, perhaps, but with no harm in him, and Constance was inclined to make rather too much fuss about the loss of her little girl.

Sir Cyprian heard this change of tone in silence, and was not convinced. He contrived to see Dr. Webb, the Maidstone surgeon, that afternoon. He remembered the good-natured little doctor as his attendant in many a childish ailment, and was not afraid of asking him a question or two. From him he heard a very bad account of Constance Sinclair. Dr. Webb professed himself fairly baffled. There was no bodily ailment, except want of strength; but there was a settled melancholy, a deep and growing depression for which medicine was of no avail.

'You'll ask why I don't propose getting a better opinion than my own,' said Dr. Webb, 'and I'll tell you why. I might call in half the great men in London and be no wiser than I am now.

They would only make Mrs. Sinclair more nervous, and she is very nervous already. I am a faithful watch-dog, and at the first indication of danger I shall take measures.'

'You don't apprehend any danger to the mind?' asked Sir Cyprian, anxiously.

'There is no immediate cause for fear. But if this melancholy contiuues, if the nervousness increases, I cannot answer for the result.'

'You have told Mr. Sinclair as much as this?'

'Yes, I have spoken to him very frankly.'

It would have been difficult to imagine a life more solitary than that which Constance Sinclair contrived to lead in a house full of guests. For the first two or three weeks she had bravely tried to sustain her part as hostess; she had pretended to be amused by the amusements of others, or, when unable to support even that poor simulation, had sat at her embroidery frame, and given the grace of her presence to the assembly. But now she was fain to hide herself all day long in her own rooms, or to walk alone in the fine old park, restricting her public appearance to the evening, when she took her place at the head of the dinner table, and endured the frivolities of the drawing-room after dinner.

Gilbert secretly resented this withdrawal, and refused to believe that the death of Baby Christabel was his wife's sole cause of grief. There was something deeper—a sorrow for the past—a regret that was intensified by Sir Cyprian's presence in the neighbourhood.

'She knows of his being at Marchbrook, of course,' Gilbert told himself. 'How do I know they have not met? She lives her own life, almost as much apart from me as if we were in separate houses. She has had time and opportunity for seeing him, and in all probability he is at March-brook only for the sake of being near her.'

But Sir Cyprian had been at Marchbrook a week, and had not seen Constance Sinclair. How the place would have reminded him of her, had not her image been always present with him in all; times and places! Every grove and meadow had its memory, every change in the fair pastoral landscape its bitter-sweet association.

Marchbrook and Davenant were divided in some parts by an eight-foot wall, in others by an oak fence. The Davenant side of the land adjoining Marchbrook was copse and wilderness, which served as covert for game. The Marchbrook side was a wide stretch of turf, which Lord Clanyarde let off as grazing land to one of his tenants. A railed in plantation here and there supported the fiction that this meadow land was a park, and for his own part Lord Clanyarde declared that he would just as soon look at oxen as at deer.

The only estimable feature of Marchbrook Park was its avenues. One of these, known as the Monk's Avenue, and supposed to have been planted in the days when Marchbrook was a Benedictine monastery, was a noble arcade of tall elms, planted a hundred feet apart, with a grassy road between them. The monastery had long vanished, leaving not a wrack behind, and the avenue now led only from wall to wall. The owners of Davenant had built a classic temple, or summer-house, at the end of this avenue, close against the boundary wall between the two estates, in order to secure the enjoyment of this vista, as it was called in the days of Horace Walpole. The windows of the summer-house looked down the wide avenue to the high road, a distance of a little more than a quarter of a mile.

This summer-house had always been a favourite resort of Mrs. Sinclair's. It overlooked the home of her youth, and she liked it on that account, for although Davenant was by far the more beautiful estate, she loved Marchbrook best.

CHAPTER XVI.

'GRIEF FILLS THE ROOM UP OF MY ABSENT CHILD.'

SIR CYPRIAN had told himself that, in coming to Marchbrook, nothing was further from his thoughts than the desire to see Constance Sinclair; yet now that he was so near her, now that he was assured of her unhappiness, the yearning for one brief meeting, one look into the sweet eyes, one pressure of the gentle hand that used to lie so trustingly in his own, grew upon him hourly, until he felt that he could not leave Marchbrook without having seen her. No motive, no thought that could have shadowed the purity of Gilbert Sinclair's wife, had his soul's desire been published to the world, blended with this yearning of Sir Cyprian's. Deepest pity and compassion moved him. Such sorrow, such loneliness as Constance Sinclair's were sacred to the man who had loved and surrendered Constance Clanyarde.

Sir Cyprian lingered at Marchbrook, and spent the greater part of his days in riding or walking over familiar ground. He was too much out of spirits to join Lord Clanyarde in the slaughter of innocent birds, and was not a little bored by that frivolous old gentleman's society in the winter evenings by the fire in the comfortable bachelor smoking-room—the one really snug apartment in that great bare house. Every night Sir Cyprian made up his mind to depart next morning; yet when morning came he still lingered.

One bright bleak day, when there were flying snowstorms and intervals of sun and blue sky, Sir Cyprian—having actually packed his portmanteau and made arrangements for being driven to the station to catch an afternoon train—took a final ramble in Marchbrook Park. He had not once put his foot on the soil that had been his, but he could get a peep at the old place across the fence. There was a melancholy pleasure in looking at those wintry glades, the young fir trees, the scudding rabbits, the screaming pheasants, the withered bracken.

The sun had been shining a few minutes ago.

Down came the snow in a thick driving shower, almost blinding Sir Cyprian, as he walked swiftly along by the oak fence. Presently he found himself at the end of the Monk's Avenue, and under that classic temple which was said to be built upon the very spot where the Benedictines once had their chapel.

Ten years ago that temple had been Cyprian Davenant's summer retreat. He had made it his smoking-room and study—had read Thucydides and the Greek dramatists there in the long vacation— had there read those books of modern travel which had fired his mind with a longing for the adventures, perils, and triumphs of the African explorer. Twenty years ago it had been his mother's chosen resort. He had spent many a summer morning, many a pensive twilight there, by his mother's side, watching her sketch or hearing her play. The old-fashioned square piano was there still, perhaps, and the old engravings on the walls.

'Poor old place,' he thought, ' I wonder if any one ever goes there now, or if it is quite given up to bats and owls, and the spirits of the dead ?'

He stopped under the stone balcony which over-hung Marchbrook, on a level with the eight-foot wall. In Gilbert Sinclair's—or his architect's—plan of improvements, this classic summer house, a relic of a departed taste, had been forgotten. Sir Cyprian was glad to find it unchanged, unchanged in any wise, save that it had a more forlorn and neglected air than of old. The stonework of the balcony was green and gray with mosses and lichens. The frame-work of the window had not been painted for a quarter of a century. The ivy had wandered as it listed over brickwork and stone, darting sharp forked tongues of green into the crevices of the decaying mortar. Sir Cyprian looked up at the well-remembered window, full of thoughts of the past.

'Does she ever come here, I wonder?' he said to himself; 'or do they use the old place for a tool-house or an apple shed?'

Hardly, for there fell upon his ear a few bars of plaintive symphony, played on a piano of ancient tone—the pensive Broadwood dear to his childhood, —and then a voice, the pure and sweet contralto he knew too well, began Lord Houghton's pathetic ballad, 'Strangers yet.'

He listened as if he lived but to hear. Oh, what profound melancholy there was in that voice, pouring out its sweetness to the silent walls! Regret, remorse, sorrow too great for common language to express, were breathed in that flood of melody. And when the song was done the singer's hands fell on the keys in a crashing chord; and a wild cry—the sudden utterance of uncontrollable despair—went up to heaven.

She was there—so near him—alone in her anguish. She, the only woman he had ever truly loved, the woman for whom he would have given his life as freely as he would have spilled a cup of water upon the ground, and with as little thought of the sacrifice.

The lower edge of the balcony was within reach of his hand. The century-old ivy would have afforded easy footing for a less skilled athlete. To climb the ascent was simple as to mount the rigging of his yacht.

In a minute, before he had time to think, he was

in the balcony, he had opened the French window, he was standing in the room!

Constance Sinclair sat by the piano, her arms folded on the old mahogany lid, her drooping head resting on her arms, her face hidden. She was too deeply lost in that agony of hopeless grief to hear the rattling of the frail casement, the footstep on the floor.

'Constance!'

She started up and confronted him, pale as ashes, with a smothered scream.

'My dearest, I heard your grief. I could not keep away. Only for a few minutes, Constance; only for a few words, and I will leave you. Oh, my love, how changed, how changed!'

A flood of crimson rushed into the pale face, and as quickly faded. Then she gave him her hand, with an innocent frankness that went to his heart, so like the Constance of old—the pure and perfect type of girlhood that knows not sin.

'I do not mind *you* hearing me in my sorrow,' she said, sadly. 'I come here because I feel myself away from all the world. At the house servants

come to my room with messages, and worry me.
Would I like this? Will I do the other? What
carriage will I drive in? at what time? A hundred
questions that are so tiresome when one is tired of
life. Here I can lock my door, and feel as much
alone as in a desert.'

'But, dear Mrs. Sinclair, it is not good for you to
abandon yourself to such grief.'

'How can I help it? "Grief fills the room up of
my absent child!"' with a sad smile. 'You heard of
my loss, did you not? The darling who made life
so bright for me—snatched away in a moment—not
one hour's warning. I woke that morning a proud
and happy mother, and at night——! No, no one
can imagine such a grief as that.'

'I have heard the sad story. But be sure Heaven
will send comfort—new hopes——'

'Don't talk to me like that. Oh, if you knew
how I have had Heaven and the Bible thrown at
my head—by people who talk by rote. I can read
my Bible. I read of David and his great despair, how
he turned his face to the wall, how he wept again
for Absalom; and of the Shunammite woman who

said, " It is well ; " but David had many children, and the Shunammite's child was given back to her. God will not give my darling back to me.'

' He will—in heaven.'

' But my heart is breaking for want of her here. She will be an angel before the throne of God—not my Christabel. I want my darling as she was on earth, with her soft clinging arms—not always good —naughty sometimes, but always dearer than my life.'

What could Sir Cyprian say to comfort this bereaved heart ? He could only sit down quietly by Constance Sinclair's side, and win her to talk of her sorrow, far more freely and confidingly than she had talked to her father ; and this he felt was something gained. There was comfort in this free speech —comfort in pouring her sorrow into the ear of a friend who could verily sympathize.

' Dear Mrs. Sinclair,' said Sir Cyprian, gravely, when he had allowed her to tell the story of her bereavement, ' as a very old friend—one who has your welfare deep at heart—I must entreat you to struggle against this aborbing grief. I have seen

Dr. Webb, and he assures me that unless you make an effort to overcome this melancholy your mind as well as your body will suffer. Yes, Constance, reason itself may give way under the burden you impose upon it. Perhaps no one else would have the courage to speak to you so plainly, but I venture to speak as a brother might to a fondly loved sister. This may be our last meeting ; for I shall go back to Africa as soon as I can get my party together again. You will try, dear friend, will you not, for my sake—for the sake of your husband——'

'My husband!' she exclaimed, with a shudder. 'He has billiards, and guns, and race-horses, and friends without number. What can it matter to him that I grieve for my child ? Somebody had need be sorry. He does not care.'

'Constance, it would matter very much to your father, to all who have ever loved you, to yourself most of all, if you should end your life in a lunatic asylum.'

This startled her, and she looked up at him earnestly.

'Unreasonable grief sometimes leads to madness.

Despair is rebellion against God. If the Shunammite in that dark day could say, "It shall be well," shall a Christian have less patience—a Christian who has been taught that those who mourn are blessed, and shall be comforted ? Yes, Constance, they shall be comforted. Have faith in that divine promise, and all will be well.'

'I will try,' she answered, gently. 'It is very good of you to reason with me. No one else has spoken so frankly. They have only talked platitudes, and begged me to divert my mind. As if acted charades, or billiards, or bézique could fill up the gap in my life. Are you really going to Africa very soon ?

'Early in the new year, perhaps ; but I shall not go till I have heard from some reliable source that you are happy.'

'You must not wait for that. I shall never know happiness again in this world. At most I can but try to bear my lot patiently, and put on cheerful looks. I shall try to do that, believe me. Your lesson shall not be wasted. And now, I suppose, we must say good-bye,' looking at her watch. 'It is time for me to go back to the house.'

'I will not detain you, but before I go I must apologize for my burglarious entrance by that window. I hope I did not frighten you.'

'I was only startled. It seemed almost a natural thing to see you here. I remember how fond you were of this summer-house when I was a child. I have so often seen you sitting in that window smoking and reading.'

'Yes, I have spent many an hour here puzzling over the choruses in "Prometheus," and I have looked up from my book to see you scamper by on your pony.'

'Pepper, the gray one,' cried Constance, absolutely smiling; 'such a dear pony! We used to feed him with bread and apples every morning. Ah, what happy days those were!'

It touched him to the core of his heart to see the old girlish look come back in all its brightness. But it was only a transient gleam of the old light, which left a deeper sadness when it faded.

'Good-bye, Constance,' he said, taking both her hands. 'I may call you that for the last time.'

'Yes, and when you are in Africa—in another

world, far from all the false pretences and sham
pleasures that make up life in this—think of me as
Constance, the Constance you knew in the days that
are gone—not as Gilbert Sinclair's wife.'

He bent his head over the unresisting hands and
kissed them.

' God bless you and comfort you, my Constance,'
he said gravely, ' and give you as much happiness
as I lost when I made up my mind to live without
you.'

He opened the window, and swung himself lightly
down from the balcony to the turf below.

CHAPTER XVII.

A BALCONY SCENE.

GILBERT SINCLAIR and his chosen set—the half-dozen turfy gentlemen with whom he was united by the closest bonds of sympathy — had ¦ spent this December morning agreeably enough at a rustic steeplechase nine miles from Davenant. The race was an event of the most insignificant order—unchronicled in Ruff,—but there was pleasure in the drive to and fro on Mr. Sinclair's drag, through the keen frosty air, with an occasional diversion in the shape of a flying snowstorm, which whitened the men's rough overcoats, and hung on their beards and whiskers.

Just at the hour in which Sir Cyprian and Constance were bidding each other a long good-bye, Mr. Sinclair was driving his sorrel team back to Davenant at a slashing pace. He and his friends had enjoyed themselves very thoroughly at the homely

farmers' meeting. The sharp north wind had given
a keen edge to somewhat jaded appetites, and game
pie, anchovy sandwiches, cold grouse, and boar's
head had been duly appreciated, with an *ad libitum*
accompaniment of dry champagne, bitter beer, and
Copenhagen Kirschen Wasser.

The gentlemen's spirits had been improved by
the morning's sport, and the homeward drive was
hilarious. It was now between three and four o'clock.
There would be time for a quiet smoke, or a game at
pyramids, and a fresh toilet before afternoon tea,
opined such of the gentlemen as still held by that
almost exploded superstition, a taste for ladies'
society. The more masculine spirits preferred to
smoke their Trabucas or Infantas by the harness-
room fire, with the chance of getting the " straight
tip " out of somebody else's groom.

James Wyatt was the only member of the party
whose spirits were not somewhat unduly elated ; but
then Mr. Wyatt was an outsider, only admitted on
sufferance into that chosen band, as a fellow who
might be useful on an emergency, and whom it was
well to " square " by an occasional burst of civility.

He was one of those dangerous men who are always sober, and who find out everybody else's weak points, without ever revealing their own. He was Sinclair's *ame damnée*, however, and one must put up with him.

Gilbert was driving, with Sir Thomas Houndslow, a gentleman of turf celebrity, and late captain of a cavalry regiment, next him, smoking furiously, while Mr. Wyatt sat behind the two, and joined freely in the conversation, which inclined to the boisterous. How calm that smooth, level voice of his sounded after the strident tones of his companions, thickened ever so slightly by champagne and Kirschen Wasser !

The chief talk was of horses—the sorrels Gilbert was now driving—the horses they had seen that morning—with an inexhaustible series of anecdotes about horses that had been bought and sold, and bred, and exchanged, including the story of a rheumatic horse, which was a splendid goer in his intervals of good health, and was periodically sold by his owner, and taken back again at half-price when the fit came on.

James Wyatt admired the landscape, an enthusiasm which his companions looked down upon contemptuously from the serene height of a stolid indifference to art and nature.

'There's a glade!' cried the solicitor, pointing to an opening in the undulating woodland, where the snow-wreathed trees were like a picture of fairyland.

'Pretty tidy timber,' assented Sir Thomas Houndslow, ' but for my part I could never see anything in trees to go into raptures about, except when you've sold 'em to a timber merchant. Shouldn't like to see cremation come into fashion, by-the-by. It would spoil the coffin trade and depreciate the value of my elms and oaks.'

As they approached Marchbrook, Mr. Wyatt began to talk about the Benedictines and their vanished monastery. He had found out all about it in the county history, its founder, the extent of its lands, the character of its architecture.

'That avenue must be six hundred years old,' he said as they came in sight of the tall elms.

'By Jove, that's queer,' cried Sir Thomas, pulling

out his race-glass. 'A fellow jumped out of that balcony like Romeo in the play.'

'Except that Romeo never scaled the balcony,' said Mr. Wyatt.

'That summer house is in your park, isn't it, Gilbert? Our friend's mode of exit suggests a flirtation between one of your guests and somebody at Marchbrook.'

'There's nobody at Marchbrook but old Clanyarde and Sir Cyprian Davenant,' said Sir Thomas, 'and I'll lay any odds you like it wasn't Lord Clanyarde jumped off that balcony.

Gilbert took the glass from his friend's hand without a word. The man who had jumped off the balcony was still in sight, walking at a leisurely pace along the wide alley of turf between the two rows of trees. The glass brought him near enough for recognition, and Mr. Sinclair had no doubt as to his identity.

'If you lay on to those leaders like that, you'll have this blessed machine in a ditch,' cried Sir Thomas Houndslow. 'What's the matter with you? The horses are stepping like clockwork.'

' Juno was breaking into a canter,' said Gilbert, colouring. ' Quiet, old lady, steady, steady.'

' *She's* steady enough,' said Sir Thomas, ' I think it's you that are wild. Memorandum, don't drink Kirschen Wasser after champagne when you're going to drive a team of young horses.'

Mr. Sinclair took the curve by the park gates in excellent style, despite this insinuation, and pulled up before the old Gothic porch with workmanlike precision.

' That's a very pretty bit of feather-edging,' said Sir Thomas, approvingly.

Gilbert did not wait to see his friends alight, but flung the reins to one of the grooms, and walked off without a word to any one.

He was at the summer-house ten minutes afterwards flushed and breathless, having run all the way. A flight of stone steps, moss-grown and broken, led up to the door of the temple.

Gilbert Sinclair tried the door, and found it locked.

' Is there any one in here?' he asked, shaking the crazy old door savagely.

'Who is that?' inquired Constance.

'Your husband.'

He heard her light footsteps coming towards the door. She opened it, and faced him on the threshold, with neither surprise nor fear in her calm, questioning face.

'Is there anything the matter, Gilbert? Am I wanted?'

'There is not much the matter, and I don't know that you are wanted in my house,' answered her husband, savagely. 'It seems to me that your vocation is elsewhere.'

His flushed face, the angry light in his red-brown eyes, told her that there was meaning in his reply, incomprehensible as it seemed.

'I don't understand you, Gilbert. What has happened to make you angry?'

'Not much, perhaps. It's bad form to make a fuss about it. But I am vulgar enough to think that when my wife plays Juliet to somebody else's Romeo it is time she should call herself by some other name than mine—which she disgraces. I admire the innocence of your astonished look. Unfortunately that

piece of finished acting is thrown away upon me. I
saw your lover leave you.'

'Mr. Sinclair!' with a look of unspeakable indignation.

'Yes, your gentle Romeo forgot that this summer-
house is seen from the high road. I saw him, I tell
you, woman—I saw him leap down from the balcony
—identified him with my field glass—not that I had
any doubt who your visitor was.'

'I am sorry that you should be so angry at my
seeing an old friend for a few minutes, Gilbert; and
that you should make so very innocent an act an
excuse for insulting me.'

'An old friend—a friend whom you meet clandestinely—in an out-of-the-way corner of the park—
with locked doors.'

'I have spent all my mornings here of late. I
lock my door in order to be undisturbed, so that
anybody happening to come this way may believe
the summer-house empty.'

'Any one except Sir Cyprian Davenant. He
would know better.'

'Sir Cyprian's presence here to-day was the

merest accident. He heard me singing, and climbed up to the balcony to say a few kind words about my bereavement, which he' knows to be the one absorbing thought of my mind just now. No friend, no brother, could have come with kinder or purer meaning. He gave me good advice, he warned me that there was selfishness and folly in giving way to sorrow. Not one word was spoken which you might not have freely heard, Gilbert, which you would not have approved.'

'Could any woman in your position say less? You all sing the same song. Once having made up your mind to betray your husband the rest is a matter of detail, and there is a miserable sameness in the details. Do you think anything you can say —oaths, tears—will ever convince me that you did not come here on purpose to meet that man, or that he came here to preach you a sermon upon your duty to me?'

'Gilbert, as I stand here, before God who sees and hears me, I have told you the truth! We have made a sad mistake in marrying; there are few things in which we sympathize; even our great sorrow has not brought us nearer together; but if you will only be patient, if you will be kind and true to me, I will still try, even more earnestly than I have done yet, to make you a good wife, to make your home life happy.'

She came to him with a sad, sweet smile, and laid her hand gently on his shoulder, looking up at him with earnest eyes, full of truth and purity, could he but have understood their meaning.

Alas! to his dogged, brutal nature, purity like this was incomprehensible. Facts were against his wife, and he had no belief in her to sustain him against the facts. The lion of fable might recognise Una's purity and lie down at her feet; but Gilbert Sinclair was a good deal more like the lion of reality, a by no means magnanimous beast, who waits till he can pounce upon his enemy alone in a solitary corner, and has a prudent dread of numbers.

As the little hand alighted tremulously on his breast Gilbert Sinclair raised his clenched fist.

'Let me alone,' he cried. 'You've made your choice. Stick to it, ——'

And then came a word which had never before

been spoken in Constance Sinclair's hearing, but which some instinct of her woman's heart told her meant deepest infamy.

She recoiled from him with a little cry, and then fell like a log at his feet.

Lest that brutal word should too weakly express an outraged husband's wrath, Mr. Sinclair had emphasized it with a blow. That muscular fist of his, trained in many an encounter with professors of the noble art of self-defence, had been driven straight at his wife's forehead, and nothing but the man's blind fury had prevented the blow being mortal.

In intention, at least, he had been for the moment a murderer. His breath came thick and fast as he stood over that lifeless form.

'Have I killed her?' he asked himself. 'She deserves no better fate. But I had rather kill *him*.'

CHAPTER XVIII.

CYPRIAN'S VISITOR.

SIR CYPRIAN DAVENANT left Marchbrook an hour after his interview with Constance Sinclair. He sent his man home with the portmanteaus and gun-cases, and went straight to his club, where he dined. It was between eight and nine when he walked to his chambers through the snowy streets. The walk through the rough weather suited his present temper. He could have walked many a mile across a Yorkshire moor that night, in the endeavour to walk down the anxious thoughts that crowded upon his mind.

His interview with Constance—like all such meetings between those whom Fate has irrevocably parted—had deepened the gloom of his soul, and added to the bitterness of his regrets. It had brought the past nearer to him, and made the inevitable harder to bear than it had seemed yesterday.

He had seen all the old loveliness in the innocent
face, changed though it was. He had heard all the
old music in the unforgotten voice. To what end?
That brief greeting across the iron gate of Destiny's
prison-house only made it more agonizing to think of
the long future in which these two, who had so met
and touched hands across the gulf, must live their
separated lives in silent patience.

The snow lay thick in the quiet turning out of
the Strand. There was a hansom standing at the
corner by Sir Cyprian's chambers, the horse hanging
his head with a dejected air under his whitened rug;
the man stamping up and down the pavement, and
flapping his arms across his chest. The cab must
have been waiting some time, Sir Cyprian thought,
idly.

His chambers were on the first floor, large and
lofty rooms facing the river. Since his inheritance
of Colonel Gryffin's fortune he had indulged himself
with that one luxury dear to men who love books, a
well-arranged library. This bachelor *pied à terre*
suited him better than lodgings in a more fashionable
quarter. It was central, and out of the way of his

fashionable acquaintance—an ineligible feature which was to his mind an attraction.

Sir Cyprian admitted himself with his latch-key, and went up the dimly lighted staircase. He opened the outer door of his library, within which massive oak barrier there hung a heavy crimson cloth curtain, shutting out noise and draught. This curtain had been dragged aside, and left hanging in a heap at one end of the rod, in a very different style from the usual neat arrangement of folds left by the middle-aged valet.

The room was almost in darkness, for the fire had burned low upon the hearth. There was just light enough to show Sir Cyprian a figure sitting by the fire in a brooding attitude, alone, and in the dark.

'Who's that?' asked Sir Cyprian.

The man started up, a big man, tall and broad-shouldered, whom for the first moment Sir Cyprian took for a stranger.

'I should have thought you would have known Constance Sinclair's husband anywhere,' said the intruder. 'You and I have good reason to remember each other.'

'I beg your pardon, Mr. Sinclair,' Cyprian answered, quietly, without noticing the sneer; 'but as I do not possess the gift of seeing in the dark you can hardly wonder at my being slow to recognise you.'

He was not going to invite a quarrel with this man—nay, he would rather avoid one even at some loss of personal dignity, for Constance's sake. He went up to the hearth, where Gilbert had resumed his seat, and put his hand on the bell.

'Don't ring for lights,' said Sinclair. 'What I have to say can be said in the dark.'

'Perhaps. But I prefer to see a man's face when I'm talking to him. May I ask to what I am indebted for this unexpected pleasure? I thought you were at Davenant.'

'I left by the train after that in which you travelled.'

The man came in with a lighted lamp, which he placed on the table in front of the fire—a large carved oak table, loaded with classic volumes and ponderous lexicons; for a wealthy student is rarely content with a single lexicographer's definition.

Having set down the lamp the valet replenished the exhausted fire with that deliberate care so frequently to be observed in a servant who is slightly curious about his master's guest, and finally retired, with soft footfall, shutting the door after him very slowly, as if he expected to gather something at this last moment from the visitor's impatience to break covert.

In this case, however, the valet retired without hearing a word. Gilbert Sinclair sat staring at the fire, and seemed in no hurry to state his business. He could not fly at his enemy's throat like a tiger; and that was about the only thing to which his spirit moved him at this moment. Looking at his visitor by the clear light of the lamp, Sir Cyprian was not reassured by his countenance. Gilbert Sinclair's face was of a livid hue, save on each high cheek bone, where a patch of dusky red made the pervading pallor more obvious. His thick red brown hair was rough and disordered, his large red-brown eyes, prominently placed in their orbits, were bright and glassy, and the sensual under lip worked convulsively, as in some inward argument of a stormy kind.

For some minutes—three or four perhaps, and so brief a space of time makes a longish pause in a critical situation—Gilbert Sinclair kept silence. Sir Cyprian, standing with his back against one end of the velvet-covered mantelpiece, waited with polite tranquillity. Not by a word or gesture did he attempt to hurry his guest.

'Look you here, Sir Cyprian Davenant,' Gilbert began at last, with savage abruptness. 'If we had lived in the duelling days—the only days when Englishmen were gentlemen—I should have sent a friend to you to-night instead of coming myself, and the business might have been arranged in the easiest manner possible, and settled decisively before break-fast to-morrow. But as our new civilization does not allow of that kind of thing, and as I haven't quite strong enough evidence to go into the Divorce Court, I thought it was better to come straight to you and give you fair warning of what you may expect in the future.'

'Let us suppose that duelling is not an exploded custom. We have France and Belgium, and a few other countries at our disposal, if we should make up our minds to fight. But I should like to know the ground of our quarrel before we go into details.'

'I am glad you are man enough to fight me,' answered the other, savagely. 'I don't think you can require to be told why I should like to kill you— or if you have been in doubt about it up to this moment you will know pretty clearly when I tell you that I saw you jump off the balcony of my wife's summer-house this afternoon.'

'I am sorry that unceremonious exit should offend you. I had no other way of getting back to Marchbrook in time for my train. I should have had to walk the whole width of Davenant Park and about a mile of high road if I had left by the summer-house door.'

'And you think it a gentlemanlike thing to be in my neighbourhood for a fortnight, to avoid my house, and to meet my wife clandestinely in a lonely corner of my park?'

'There was no clandestine meeting. You insult your wife by such a supposition, and prove—if proof were needed of so obvious a fact—your unworthiness of such a wife. My visit to the summer-house was

purely accidental.   I heard Mrs. Sinclair singing—
heard the bitter cry which grief—a mother's sacred
grief—wrung from her in her solitude, and followed
the impulse of the moment, which prompted me to
console a lady whom I knew and loved when she
was a child.'

'And afterwards, when she had ceased to be a
child—a few months before she became my wife.
Your attachment was pretty well known to the world
in general, I believe.   It was only I who was left in
ignorance.'

'You might easily have known what the world
knew—all there was to be known—simply nothing.'

'You deny that you have done me any wrong?
that I have any right to ask you to fight me?'

'Most emphatically, and I most distinctly refuse
to make a quarrel on any ground connected with
your wife.   But you will not find me slow to resent
an insult should you be so ill-advised as to provoke
me.   As the friend of Constance Clanyarde I shall
be very ready to take up the cudgels for Constance
Sinclair, even against her husband.   Remember this,
Mr. Sinclair; and remember that any wrong done to

Lord Clanyarde's daughter will be a wrong that I shall revenge with all the power God has given me. She is not left solely to her husband's tender mercies.'

Even the dull red hue faded from Gilbert Sinclair's cheeks as he confronted the indignant speaker, and left him livid to the very lips. There was a dampness on his forehead, too, when he brushed his large strong hand across it.

'Is the man a craven?' thought Sir Cyprian, remarking these signs of agitation.

'Well,' said Sinclair, drawing a long breath, 'I suppose there is no more to be said. You both tell the same story—an innocent meeting, not preconcerted—mere accident. Yes, you have the best of me this time. The unlucky husband generally has the worst of it. There's no dishonour in lying to *him*. He's out of court, poor beggar.'

'Mr. Sinclair, do you want me to throw you out of that window?'

'I shouldn't much care if you did.'

There was a sullen misery in the answer, and in the very look and attitude of the man as he sat

beside his enemy's hearth, only looking up at intervals from his vacant stare at the fire, which touched
Cyprian Davenant with absolute pity.   Here was a
man to whom Fate had given vast capabilities of
happiness, and who had wantonly thrown away all
that is fairest and best in life.

'Mr. Sinclair, upon my honour I am sorry for
you,' he said, gravely.   'I am sorry for your inca-
pacity to believe in a noble and pure-minded wife;
sorry that you should poison your own life and your
wife's by doubts that would never enter your mind
if you had the power to understand her.   Go home,
and let your wife never know the wrong you have
done her.'

'My wife!   What wife ?   I have no wife,' said
Sinclair, with a strange smile, rising and going to the
door.   'That's what some fellow says in a play, I
think.   Good night, Sir Cyprian Davenant, and when
next we meet I hope it may be on a better defined
footing.'

He left the room without another word.   Before
Sir Cyprian's bell had summoned the smooth-faced
valet, the street door shut with a bang, and Gilbert

Sinclair was gone. Sir Cyprian heard the doors of the hansom clapped to, and the crack of the weary driver's whip, as the wheels rolled up the silent street.

'What did he mean by that speech about his wife?' wondered Sir Cyprian. 'The man looked like a murderer.'

He did not know that at this moment Gilbert Sinclair was half afraid that brutal blow of his might have been fatal.

CHAPTER XIX.

MRS. WALSINGHAM BREAKS FAITH.

CHRISTMAS, which, in a common way, brings life and bustle and the gathering of many guests to good old country houses, brought only gloom and solitude to Davenant. Mr. Sinclair's visitors had departed suddenly, at a single flight, like swallows before a storm in autumn. Mrs. Sinclair was very ill—seriously ill —mysteriously ill. Her dearest friends shook their heads and looked awful things when they talked of her. It was mental, they feared.

'Poor dear thing! This comes of Lord Clanyarde's greediness in getting rich husbands for all his daughters.'

'The old man is a regular harpy,' exclaimed Mrs. Millamount, with a charming indifference to detail.

And then these fashionable swallows skimmed away to fresh woods and pastures new—or rather fresh billiard-rooms—and other afternoon teas, evening part-songs, and morning rides in rustic English lanes, where there is beauty and fragrance even in mid-winter.

Constance had been missing at afternoon tea on the day of Gilbert's sudden journey to London, but her absence in the cosy morning-room, where Mrs. Millamount amused the circle by the daring eccentricity of her discourse, was hardly a subject of wonder.

'She has one of her nervous headaches, no doubt, poor child,' said Mrs. Millamount, taking possession of the tea-tray; 'she is just the kind of woman to have nervous headaches.'

'I'll give long odds you don't have them,' said Sir Thomas Houndslow, who was lolling with his back against the mantelpiece, to the endangerment of the porcelain that adorned it.

'Never had headache but once in my life, and that was when I came a cropper in the Quorn country,' replied Mrs. Millamount, graciously.

Vapours have given way to feminine athletics, and there is nothing now so dowdy or unfashionable as bad health.

When the dressing-bell rang and Mrs. Sinclair was still absent, Melanie Duport began to think there was some cause for alarm. Her mistress was punctual and orderly in all her habits. She had gone to walk in the park immediately after luncheon, quite three hours ago. She had no idea of going beyond the park, Melanie knew, as she only wore her seal-skin jacket and a garden hat. She might have gone to Marchbrook, perhaps, in this careless attire, but not anywhere else; and her visits to Marchbrook were very rare.

Melanie was puzzled. She went downstairs and sent a couple of grooms in quest of her mistress. The gardeners had all gone home at five o'clock.

'You had better look in the summer-house by the fir plantation,' said Melanie; 'I know Mrs. Sinclair spends a good deal of her time there.'

The young men took the hint, and went straight off to the summer-house together, too social to take different directions, as Melanie had told them to do. They had plenty to talk about, the furious pace at which their master was going, the bad luck which had attended his racing stable lately, and so on.

'I think there's a curse on them buildings at Newmarket,' said one of the men. 'We haven't pulled off so much as a beggarly plate since they was finished.'

'There's a curse on buying half-bred colts,' retorted the older and wiser servant. 'That's where the curse is, Rogers, mistaken economy.'

The classic temple was wrapped in darkness, and Rogers, who entered first, stumbled over the prostrate form of his mistress. She lay just as she had fallen at her husband's feet, felled by his savage blow.

The elder man got a light out of his fusee box, and then they lifted the senseless figure into a chair, and looked at the white face, on which there were ghastly streaks of blood. Mrs. Sinclair groaned faintly as they raised her from the ground, and this was a welcome sound, for they had almost thought her dead.

There were some flowers in a vase on the table, and the elder groom dipped a handkerchief in the water and dabbed it on Mrs. Sinclair's forehead.

'I wish I'd got a drop of spirit in my pocket,' he

said; 'a sup of brandy might bring her round, perhaps. Look about if you can see anything in that
way, Rogers.'

Rogers looked, but alcohol being an unknown
want to Mrs. Sinclair, there was no convenient
bottle to be found in the summer-house. She murmured something inarticulate; and the locked lips
loosened and trembled faintly as the groom bathed
her forehead.

"Poor thing, she must have had a fit,' said the
elder man.

' Apocalyptic, perhaps,' suggested Rogers.

' We'd better carry her back to the house between
us. She's only a feather weight, poor little thing.'

So the two grooms conveyed Mrs. Sinclair gently
and carefully back to Davenant, and contrived to carry
her up to her room by the servants' staircase without
letting all the house into the secret.

' If it was a fit she won't like it talked about,'
said the head groom to the housekeeper, as he re-
freshed himself with a glass of Glenlivat after his
exertions.

' Master's gone up to London, too,' said the housekeeper; 'that makes it awkward, don't it? I should think somebody ought to telegraph.'

Melanie Duport took charge of her mistress with a self-possession that would have done credit to an older woman.

She sent off at once for Dr. Webb, who came post haste to his most important patient.

The doctor found Mrs. Sinclair weak and low, and her mind wandering a little. He was much puzzled by that contusion on the fair forehead, but his patient could give him no explanation.

'I think I fell,' she said. 'It was kind of him to come to me, wasn't it, for the love of old times?'

'It must have been a very awkward fall,' said Dr. Webb to Melanie. 'Where did it happen?'

Melanie explained how her mistress had been found in the summer-house.

'She must have fallen against some piece of furniture—something with a blunt edge. It was an awful blow. She is very low, poor thing. The system has received a severe shock.'

And then Dr. Webb enjoined the greatest care, and questioned Melanie as to her qualifications for

the post of nurse. Mrs. Sinclair was not to be left
during the night, and some one else must be got to-
morrow to relieve Melanie. It was altogether a
serious case.

Gilbert Sinclair returned next morning, haggard
and gloomy, looking like a man who had spent his
night at the gaming-table, with fortune steadily
adverse to him. He met Dr. Webb in the hall, and
was told that his wife was seriously ill.

' Not in danger ? ' he asked, eagerly.

' Not in immediate danger.'

' I thank God for that.'

It seemed a small thing to be thankful for, since
the surgeon's tone was not very hopeful, but Gilbert
Sinclair had been weighed down by the apprehension
of something worse than this. He found James
Wyatt alone in the billiard-room, and learned from
him that his guests were already on the wing.

Three days later and Mr. Wyatt had also left
Davenant, but not for good. He had promised to run
down again in a week or so, to cheer his dear friend.
who, although always treating him more or less
de havt en bas, allowed him to see pretty plainly that

he was indispensable to his patron's contentment. And your modern Umbra will put up with a good deal of snubbing when he knows his patron is under his thumb.

Unfashionable as was the season, Mrs. Walsingham was still in town. She had no rustic retreat of her own, and she was not in that charmed circle, patrician or millionaire, which rejoices in country houses. Furthermore she abhorred the beauties of nature, and regarded winter residence in the country as an exile bleaker than Ovid's banishment to chill and savage Tomi. If she had been rich enough to have indulged her caprices, she would have liked to spend the New Year in Paris; but she had an income which just enabled her to live elegantly without any indulgence of caprices. This winter, too, she had peculiar reasons for staying in town, over and above all other motives. She stayed in the snug little house in Half-moon Street, therefore, and was 'at home' on Saturday evenings just as if the season had been at its flood. The society with which she filled her miniature drawing-room was literary, musical, artistic, dramatic, just the most delightful society imaginable, with the faintest flavour of Bohemianism. She had chosen Saturday evening, because journalists, who were free on no other night, could drop in then, and Mrs. Walsingham adored journalists.

On this particular Saturday, three days after the scene in the summer-house, James Wyatt had made his appearance in the Half-moon Street drawing-room just when most people were going away. He contrived to outstay them all, though Mrs. Walsingham's manner was not so cordial as to invite him to linger. She yawned audibly behind the edge of her large black fan when Mr. Wyatt took up his stand in front of the chimney-piece, with the air of a man who is going to be a fixture for the next hour.

'Have you heard the news?' he asked, after a brief silence.

'From Davenant? Yes, I am kept pretty well *au courant.*'

'A sharp little thing, that Duport.'

'Very.'

Silence again, during which Mrs. Walsingham

surveyed her violet velvet gown and admired the Venice point flounce which relieved its sombre hue.

'Clara,' said James Wyatt, with a suddenness which startled the lady into looking up at him, 'I think I have performed my part of our bargain. When are you going to perform yours?'

'I don't quite understand you.'

'Oh, yes, you do, Mrs. Walsingham. There are some things that will hardly bear to be discussed, even between conspirators. I am not going to enter into details. When I found you in this room three years ago, on Gilbert Sinclair's wedding day, you had but one thought, one desire. Your whole being was athirst for revenge. You are revenged, and I have been the chief instrument in the realization of your wish. A wicked wish on your part. Doubly wicked on mine, with less passion and weaker hatred, to be your aider and abettor. *Soit.* I am content to bear the burden of my guilt, but not to be cheated of my reward. What I have done I have done for your sake—to win your love.'

'To buy me,' she said, 'as slaves are bought with a price. That's what you mean. You don't suppose I shall love you for working Gilbert Sinclair's ruin?'

'You wanted to see him ruined.'

'Yes, when I was mad with rage and grief. Did you think you were talking to a sane woman that evening after Gilbert's marriage? You were talking to a woman whose brain had been on fire with despair and jealousy through the long hours of that agonizing day. What should I long for *but* revenge, *then?*'

'Well, you have had your heart's desire, and it seems to me that your conduct since that day has been pretty consistent with the sentiments you gave expression to then. Do you mean to tell me that you are going to throw me over now,—that you are going to repudiate the promise you made me—a promise on which I have counted with unflinching faith in your honour?'

In my honour!' cried Mrs. Walsingham, with a bitter sneer, all the more bitter because it was pointed against herself. 'In the honour of a woman who could act as I have acted?'

'I forgive anything to passion; but to betray *me* would be deliberate cruelty.'

'Would it?' she asked, smiling at him; 'I think it would be more cruel to keep my word and make your life miserable.'

'You shall make me as miserable as you please, if you will only have me,' urged Wyatt. 'Come, Clara, I have been your slave for the last three years. I have sacrificed sentiments which most men hold sacred to serve or to please you. It would be unparalleled baseness to break your promise.'

'My promise was wrung from me in a moment of blind passion,' cried Mrs. Walsingham. 'If the Prince of Darkness had asked me to seal a covenant with him that day, I should have consented as freely as I consented to your bargain.'

'The comparison is flattering to me,' replied Mr. Wyatt, looking at her darkly from under bent brows. There is a stage at which outraged love turns to keenest hate, and James Wyatt's feelings were fast approaching that stage. 'In one word, do you mean to keep faith with me? Yes or no?'

'No,' answered Mrs. Walsingham, with a steady look which meant defiance. 'No, and again no. Tell the world what you have done, and how I have cheated you. Publish your wrongs if you dare. I have never loved but one man in my life, and his name is Gilbert Sinclair. And now good night, Mr. Wyatt, or rather, good morning, for it is Sunday, and I don't want to be late for church.'

CHAPTER XX.

DR. HOLLENDORF.

THE new year began with much ringing of parish bells, some genuine joviality in cottages and servants' halls, and various conventional rejoicings in polite society; but silence and solitude still reigned at Davenant. The chief rooms—saloon and dining-room, library and music-room—were abandoned altogether by the gloomy master of the house. They might as well have put on their holland pinafores and shut their shutters, as in the absence of the family, for nobody used them. Gilbert Sinclair lived in his snuggery at the end of the long gallery, ate and drank there, read his newspapers and wrote his letters, or smoked and dozed in the dull winter evenings. He rode a good deal in all kinds of weather, going far afield, no one knew where, and coming home at dusk splashed to the neck, and with his horse in a condition peculiarly aggravating to grooms and stable boys.

'Them there 'osses will 'ave mud fever before long,' said the hirelings, dejectedly. 'There's that blessed chestnut he set such store by a month ago with 'ardly a leg to stand on for windgalls, and the roan filly's over at knee a'ready.'

'He' meant Mr. Sinclair, who was riding his finest horses with a prodigal recklessness.

Constance Sinclair lived to see the new year, though she did not know why the church bells rang out on the silence of midnight. She started up from her pillow with a frightened look when she heard that joy-peal, crying out that those were her wedding bells, and that she must get ready for church.

'To please you, papa,' she said. 'For your sake, papa. Pity my broken heart.'

There had been days and nights, towards the end of the old year, when Dr. Webb trembled for the sweet young life which he had watched almost from its beginning. A great physician had come down from London every day, and had gone away with a fee proportionate to his reputation, after diagnosing and prognosing the disease in a most wonderful manner, but it was the little country apothecary who

saved Constance Sinclair's life. His watchfulness, his
devotion, had kept the common enemy at bay. The
life current, which had ebbed very low, flowed gradu-
ally back, and, after lying for ten days in an utterly
prostrate and apathetic state, the patient was now
strong enough to rise and be dressed, and lie on the
sofa in her pretty morning-room, while Melanie, or
honest Martha Briggs, who had come back to nurse
her old mistress, read to her, to divert her mind,
the doctor said; but, alas! as yet the mind seemed
incapable of being awakened to interest in the
things of this mortal life. When Constance spoke
it was of the past—of her childhood or girlhood,
of people and scenes familiar to her in that
happy time. Of her husband she never spoke;
and his rare visits to her room had a disturbing
influence. So obvious was the disquietude caused
by his presence, that Dr. Webb suggested that for
the present Mr. Sinclair should refrain from seeing
his wife.

'I can feel for you, my dear sir,' he said, sympathetically. 'I quite understand your anxiety, but
you may trust me and the nurses. You will have

all intelligence of progress. The mind at present is somewhat astray.'

'Do you think it will be always so?' asked Sinclair. 'Will she never recover her senses?'

'My dear sir, there is everything to hope. She is so young, and the disease is altogether so mysterious; whether the effect of the blow—that unlucky fall—or whether simply a development of the brooding melancholy which we had to fight against before the accident, it is impossible to say. We are quite in the dark. Perfect seclusion and tranquillity may do much.'

Lord Clanyarde came to see his daughter nearly every day. He had stayed at Marchbrook on purpose to be near her. But his presence seemed to give Constance no pleasure. There were days on which she looked at him with a wandering gaze that went to his heart, or a blank and stony look that appalled him by its awful likeness to death. There were other days when she knew him; on those days her talk was all of the past, and it was clear that memory had taken the place of intelligence.

Lord Clanyarde felt all the pangs of remorse as

he contemplated this spectacle of a broken heart—a mind wrecked by sorrow.

'Yet I can hardly blame myself for her sad state, poor child,' he argued. 'She was happy enough, bright enough, before she lost her baby.'

The new year was a week old, and since that first rally there had been no change for the better in Constance Sinclair's condition, and now there came a decided change for the worse. Strength dwindled, a dull apathy took possession of the patient, and even memory seemed a blank.

Dr. Webb was in despair, and fairly owned his helplessness. The London physician came and went, and took his fee, and went on diagnosing with profoundest science, and tried the last resources of the pharmacopœia, with an evident conviction that he could minister to a mind diseased; but nothing came of his science, save that the patient grew daily weaker, as if fate and physic were too much for one feeble sufferer to cope withal.

Gilbert Sinclair was told that unless a change came very speedily his wife must die.

'If we could rouse her from this apathetic state,'

said the physician—' any shock—any surprise—
especially of a pleasurable kind—that would act on
the torpid brain, might do wonders even yet; but
all our attempts to interest her have so far been
useless.'

Lord Clanyarde was present when this opinion
was pronounced. He went home full of thought—
more deeply concerned for his daughter than he had
ever been yet for any mortal except himself.

'Poor little Connie,' he thought, remembering her
in her white frock and blue sash, ' she was always
my favourite—the prettiest, the gentlest, the most
high-bred of all my girls; but I didn't know she had
such a hold upon my heart.'

At Marchbrook Lord Clanyarde found an unexpected visitor waiting for him—a visitor whom he
received with a very cordial greeting.

＊　＊　＊　＊　＊　＊

Soon after dusk on the following evening Lord
Clanyarde returned to Davenant, but not alone. He
took with him an elderly gentleman, with white
hair, worn rather long, and a white beard—a person
of almost patriarchal appearance, but somewhat

disfigured by a pair of smoke-coloured spectacles of the kind that are vulgarly known as gig lamps.

The stranger's clothes were of the shabbiest, yet even in their decay looked the garments of a gentleman. He wore ancient shepherd's plaid trousers, and a bottle-green overcoat of exploded cut.

Gilbert Sinclair was in the hall when Lord Clanyarde and his companion arrived. Mr. Wyatt had just come down from London, and the two men were smoking their cigars by the great hall fire—the noble open hearth with brazen dogs, which had succeeded the more mediæval fashion of a fire in the centre of the hall.

'My dear Sinclair,' began Lord Clanyarde, with a somewhat hurried and nervous air, which might be forgiven in a man whose favourite daughter languished between life and death, 'I have ventured to bring an old friend of mine, Dr. Hollendorf, a gentleman who has a great practice in Berlin, and who has had vast experience in the treatment of mental disorders. Dr. Hollendorf—Mr. Sinclair. I beg your pardon, Wyatt, how do ye do?' interjected Lord Clanyarde, offering the solicitor a couple of

fingers. 'Now, Gilbert, I should much like Dr.
Hollendorf to see my poor Constance. It may do
no good, but it can do no harm; and if you have no
objection, with Dr. Webb's concurrence, of course, I
should like——'

'Webb is in the house,' answered Gilbert. 'You
can ask him for yourself. I have no objection.'

This was said with a weary air, as if the speaker
had ceased to take any interest in life.   Gilbert
hardly looked at the German doctor; but James
Wyatt, who was of a more observant turn, scruti-
nized him attentively.

'Here is Webb,' said Gilbert, as the little doctor
came tripping down the great staircase, with the
lightsome activity of his profession, washing his
hands, in imaginary water, like Lady Macbeth, as
he came.

Lord Clanyarde presented Dr. Hollendorf to the
rural practitioner, and stated his wish.   Dr. Webb
had no objection to offer.   Any wish of a father's
must be sacred.

'You will come up and see her at once?' he
said, interrogatively.

'At once,' answered the stranger, with a slightly guttural accent.

The three men went up the staircase, Gilbert remaining behind.

'Aren't you going?' asked Wyatt.

'No, my presence generally disturbs her. Why should I go? I'm not wanted.'

'I should go if I were you. How do you know what this man is? An impudent quack in all probability. You ought to be present.'

'Do you think so?'

'Decidedly.'

'Then I'll go.'

'Watch your wife when that man is talking to her,' said Wyatt, in a lower tone, as Gilbert moved away.

'What do you mean?' asked the other, turning sharply round.

'What I say. Watch your wife.'

Mrs. Sinclair's morning-room was a spacious old-fashioned apartment, with three long windows, one opening into a wide balcony from which an iron stair led down to a small and secluded garden, laid out in the Dutch style, a garden which had been always sacred to the mistress of Davenant. There were heavy oak shutters, and a complicated arrangement of bolts and bars to the three windows; but, as these shutters were rarely closed, the stair and the balcony might be considered as a convenience specially provided for the benefit of burglars. No burglars had, however, yet been heard of at Davenant.

There was a piano in the room. There were well-filled bookcases, pictures, quaint old china—all things that make life pleasant to the mind that is at ease, and which may be supposed to offer some consolation to the care-burdened spirit. The fire blazed merrily, and on a sofa in front of it Constance reclined, dressed in a loose white cashmere gown, hardly whiter than the wasted oval face, from which the dark brown hair was drawn back by a band of blue ribbon, just as it had been ten years ago, when Constance was 'little Connie,' flitting about the lawn at Marchbrook like a white and blue butterfly.

'My pet,' said Lord Clanyarde, in a pleading tone, 'I have brought a new doctor to see you, a gentleman who may be able to understand your case even better than our friend Webb.'

'No one ever knew her constitution as well as I do,' commented Dr. Webb, *sotto voce*.

Constance raised her heavy eyelids and looked at her father with a languid wonder, as if the figures standing by her couch were far away, and she saw them faintly in the distance without knowing what they were.

The new doctor did not go through the usual formula of pulse and tongue, nor did he ask the old established questions, but he seated himself quietly by Constance Sinclair's sofa and began to talk to her in a low voice, while Dr. Webb and Lord Clanyarde withdrew to the other end of the room, where Gilbert was standing by a table, absently turning over the leaves of a book.

'You have had a great sorrow, my dear lady,' said the German doctor, in that low and confidential tone which sometimes finds its way to the clouded brain when a louder utterance conveys no meaning.

'You have had a great sorrow, and have given

way to grief, as if there were no comfort either in earth or in heaven.'

Constance listened with lowered eyelids, but a look of attention came into her face presently, which the doctor perceived.

'Dear lady, there is always comfort in heaven—there is sometimes consolation on earth. Why can you not hope for some sudden, unlooked-for happiness, some great joy such as God has sometimes given to mourners like you? Your child was drowned, you think. What if you were deceived when you believed in her death? What if she was saved from the river? I do not say that it is so, but you cannot be certain. Who can know for a certainty that the little one was really drowned?'

The eyes were wide open now, staring at him wildly.

'What's the old fellow about so long?' asked Gilbert, impatiently.

'He is talking to her about her child,' replied Lord Clanyarde. 'He wants to make her cry if he can. He's a great psychologist.'

'Does that mean a great humbug?' asked Gilbert.
'It sounds like it.'

'Hope and comfort are coming to you, dear Mrs. Sinclair,' said the German doctor, 'be sure of that.'

Again Constance looked at him curiously; but at sight of the smoke-coloured spectacles and the sallow old face, half covered with white hair, she turned away her eyes with a sigh. If she could have seen eyes that looked honestly into hers, it might have given force to that promise of comfort, but this blind oracle was too mysterious. She gave a long sigh, and answered nothing.

The doctor looked at the open piano on the other side of the fireplace, and remained in thoughtful silence for a few moments.

'Does your mistress sing sometimes?' he asked Martha Briggs, who sat on guard by the sofa.

'No, sir, not since she's been so ill, but she plays sometimes, by snatches, beautiful. It would go to your heart to hear her.'

'Will you sing to me?' asked the doctor, 'if you are strong enough to go to the piano. Pray, try to sing.'

Constance looked at him with the same puzzled gaze, and then tried to rise. Martha supported her on one side, the doctor on the other, as she feebly tottered to the piano.

'I'll sing if you like,' she said, in a careless tone that told how far the mind was from consciousness of the present. 'Papa likes to hear me sing.'

She seated herself at the piano, and her fingers wandered slowly over the keys—and wandered on in a dreamy prelude that had little meaning. The German doctor listened patiently for a few minutes to this tangle of arpeggios, and then bending over the piano, played the few notes of a familiar symphony.

Constance gave a faint cry of surprise, and then she struck a chord—the chord that closed the symphony, and began, 'Strangers yet,' in a voice that had a strange hysterical power which was in curious contrast with the feebleness of the singer.

She sang on till she came to the words, 'Child and parent.' These touched a sensitive chord. She rose suddenly from the piano and burst into tears.

'That may do good,' said Dr. Webb, approvingly.

'My friend is no fool,' replied Lord Clanyarde.

'Take your mistress to her room,' said Gilbert to Martha, with an angry look. 'This is only playing upon her nerves. I wonder you can allow such folly, Lord Clanyarde.'

'Your own doctors have agreed that some shock was necessary, something to awaken her from apathy. Poor pet, those tears are a relief,' answered the father.

He went to his daughter and assisted in arranging the pillows as she lay down on the sofa. Martha calmly ignored her master's order.

The German doctor bent over Mrs. Sinclair for a moment, and whispered the one word 'Hope,' and then retired with the three other gentlemen.

'Would you like to prescribe anything?' asked Dr. Webb, taking the stranger into a little room off the hall.

'No, it is a case in which drugs are useless. Hope is the only remedy for Mrs. Sinclair's disease. She must be beguiled with hope, even if it be delusive.'

'What?' cried Dr. Webb, 'would you trifle with

her feelings ?—play upon the weakness of her mind, and let her awaken by-and-by to find herself deluded ? '

' I would do anything to snatch her from the jaws of death,' answered the German doctor, unhesitatingly. ' If hope is not held out to her, she will die. You see her fading day by day. Do you think there is any charm in your medicines that will bring her back to life ? '

' I fear not, sir,' answered Dr. Webb, despondently.

' Then you, or those who love her, must find some more potent influence. She is heart-broken for the loss of her child. She must be taught to think that her child is still living.'

' But when her mind grows stronger it would be a still heavier blow to discover that she had been deceived.'

' She would be better able to bear the blow when health and strength had returned; and she might have formed an attachment in the meantime which would console her in the hour of disillusion.'

' I don't understand,' faltered Dr. Webb.

'I'll make myself clearer. A child must be brought to Mrs. Sinclair, a little girl of about the age of her own baby, and she must be persuaded to believe, now while her brain is clouded, that her own child is given back to her.'

'A cruel deception,' cried Dr. Webb.

'No; only a desperate remedy. Which are her friends to do, deceive her, or let her die? In her present condition of mind she will ask no questions, she will not speculate upon probabilities. She will take the child to her breast as a gift from heaven. A mind distraught is always ready to believe in the marvellous, to imagine itself the object of supernatural intervention.'

Dr. Webb looked thoughtful and half convinced. This German physician, who spoke very good English, by the way, seemed to have studied his subject deeply. Dr. Webb was no psychologist; but he had seen in the mentally afflicted that very love of the marvellous which Dr. Hollendorf spoke about. And what hope had he of saving his patient? Alas! none. It would be a cruel thing to put a spurious child in her arms—to trifle with a

mother's sacred feelings ; but if life and reason could
be saved by this means, and no other, surely the
fraud would be a pious one.

'Mr. Sinclair would never consent,' said Dr. Webb.

'Mr. Sinclair must be made to consent.   I have
already suggested this step to Lord Clanyarde, and
he approves the idea.   He must bring his influence
to bear upon Mr. Sinclair, who appears an indifferent
husband, and not warmly interested in his wife's
fate.'

'There you wrong him,' cried the faithful Webb.
'His manner does not do him justice.   The poor
man has been in a most miserable condition ever
since Mrs. Sinclair's illness assumed an alarming
aspect.   Will you make this suggestion to him—
propose our introducing a strange child ? '

'I would rather the proposal should come from
Lord Clanyarde,' answered the strange doctor, looking at his watch.   'I must get back to London by
the next train.   I shall tell Lord Clanyarde my
opinion as he drives me to the station.   I think I
have made my ideas sufficiently clear to you, Dr.
Webb ?'

'Quite so, quite so,' cried the little man, whose mother was an Aberdeen woman. 'It is a most extraordinary thing, Dr. Hollendorf, that although I have never had the honour of meeting you before, your voice is very familiar to me.'

'My dear sir, do you suppose that nature can give a distinctive voice to every unit in an over-crowded world ? You might hear my voice in the Fijis to-morrow. There would be nothing extra-ordinary in that.'

'Quite so. An accidental resemblance,' assented Dr. Webb.

The German would take no fee ; he had come as Lord Clanyarde's friend, and he drove away in Lord Clanyarde's brougham, without any further loss of time.

Gilbert Sinclair and his solicitor devoted the rest of the evening to billiards, with frequent refresh-ment on Gilbert's part in the way of brandy and soda.

'You talked the other day about finding a pur-chaser for this confounded old barrack,' said Mr. Sinclair. 'I hate the place more every day, and it is

costing me no end of money for repairs ; never saw
such a rickety old hole—always some wall tumbling
down, or drain getting choked up—to say nothing
of keeping up a large stable here as well as at Newmarket.'

'Why not give up Newmarket ?' suggested Mr.
Wyatt, with his common-sense air.

'I am not such a fool.   Newmarket gives me
some pleasure, and this place gives me none.'

'You must keep up a home for Mrs. Sinclair ;
and a London house would hardly be suitable in her
present state.'

'I can take her to Hastings, or Ventnor, or to my
box at Newmarket, if it comes to that.'

'Isn't it better for her to be near her father ?'

'What does she want with her father, an old
twaddler like Clanyarde, without a thought beyond
the gossip of his club? Don't humbug, Wyatt. You
told me you could put your finger on a purchaser.
Was that bosh, or did you mean it ?'

'It was not bosh,' answered Wyatt, 'but I wanted
to be quite sure you were in earnest before I pushed
my proposal any further. You might consider it

an impertinence even for me to think of such a thing.'

'What are you driving at ?'

'Will you sell Davenant to me ?'

Gilbert dropped his billiard cue, and stood staring at his friend in blank amazement. Here was a new state of things indeed. The professional man treading on the heels of the millionaire.

'You!' he exclaimed, with contemptuous surprise. 'I did not think fifteen per cent. and renewals could be made so profitable.'

'I am too thick-skinned to resent the insinuation,' said James Wyatt, cushioning his opponent's ball. 'I can afford to buy Davenant at the price you gave for it. I've got just enough money disengaged—I sold out of Palermos the other day when they were up—to provide the purchase-money. I brought down a deed of transfer, and if you are in earnest we can settle the business to-morrow morning.'

'You're buying the place as a speculation ?' said Gilbert, suspiciously.

'Not **exactly.** But what would it matter to you

if I were ? You want to get rid of the place. I
am ready to take it off your hands.'

'You have heard of a bid from somebody else?'

'No, I have not.'

'Well, you're a curious fellow! Going to get
married, I suppose, and turn country squire?'

'Never mind my plans. Do you mean to sell?'

'Yes.'

'Then I am ready to buy.'

The deed was executed next morning. Gilbert
stipulated that he was not to surrender the house
till the Midsummer quarter, and that James Wyatt
was to take the furniture and give him something
handsome for his improvements.

Mr. Sinclair was much pleased at the idea of
getting back five-and-thirty thousand pounds of
ready money for a place the purchase of which had
been a whim, and of the occupation whereof he was
heartily tired. Those miners in the north were still
holding out, and money had not been flowing into
his coffers nearly so fast as it had been flowing out
during the last half-year. He had made unlucky
bargains in horse-flesh—squandered his money on

second-rate stock—and on running small races that were not worth his people's travelling expenses. In a word, he had done all those foolish things which an idle man who thinks himself extremely clever, and yet lends an ear to every new adviser, is apt to do.

'Five-and-thirty thou' will put me into smooth water,' he said, as he signed the contract with a flourish.

The one suspicion as to Mr. Wyatt's intentions, which would have prevented Gilbert Sinclair agreeing to the bargain, had never presented itself to his mind.

James Wyatt went back to London that afternoon, promising to meet his client next day at the Argyle Street branch of the Union Bank, and hand over the purchase-money. At eight o'clock that evening he presented himself at Sir Cyprian Davenant's chambers. He found Cyprian sitting alone among his books, smoking an Indian hookah.

'Wyatt, old fellow,' this is a surprise,' said Cyprian, as they shook hands. 'Have you dined?'

'Thanks, yes, I took a chop at the Garrick. I've just come from Davenant.'

'Indeed ! How is Mrs. Sinclair ?'

' Pretty much the same, poor soul. How long is it since you heard of her ?'

' I saw Lord Clanyarde at his club about a week ago.'

'Well, there's been no change lately. Something wrong with the mind, you see, and a gradual ebbing away of strength. She's not long for this world, I'm afraid ; but she was too good for it. Angels are better off in heaven than they are with us. We don't appreciate them.'

'No more than swine appreciate pearls,' said Sir Cyprian.

'What would you give to get Davenant back ?' asked Mr. Wyatt, without preface.

'What would I give ? Anything—half my fortune.'

'What is your fortune worth ?'

'About a hundred and fifty thousand.'

'Well, then, I shan't want so much as half of it, though your offer is tempting. Davenant is mine.'

' Yours ! '

' Yes, at the price you got for it, with another five thousand as a sporting bid for the furniture and improvements. Give me five-and-twenty per cent. on my purchase, and Davenant is yours.'

' Willingly. But how about Mrs. Sinclair ? Will it not grieve her to lose the place ?'

' Whether or no, the place is sold. I tell you, Sir Cyprian, I stand before you the owner of Davenant and all its appurtenances. I did not buy it for myself, but on the speculation that, as I bought it cheap, you would be glad to give me a profit on my purchase. I knew Sinclair well enough to be very sure that he would let the roof rot over his head before he would consent to sell the place to you.'

' You have done a friendly thing, Wyatt, and I thank you. I should hesitate, perhaps, in agreeing to such a bargain were any other man than Mr. Sinclair in question, but I do not feel myself bound to stand upon punctilio with him.'

' Punctilio, man ! There's no punctilio to stand upon. Sinclair sold the estate to me unconditionally, and I have an indisputable right to sell it to you.'

CHAPTER XXI.

A RAPID THAW.

SIR CYPRIAN DAVENANT had ridden to Totteridge several times after his discovery of Mrs. Walsingham's connection with the village, as tenant of that small and unpretending house with the green shutters, glass door, and square plot of garden. It was his habit to put up his horse at the inn, and go for a rustic stroll while the animal rested after his mid-day feed, and in these rambles he had made the acquaintance of the nurse and baby at the green-shuttered house.

The nurse was a German girl, fat-faced, good-natured, and unintelligent. Sir Cyprian won her heart at the outset by addressing her in her native language, which she had not heard since she came to England, and in the confidence inspired by his kind manners and excellent German she freely imparted her affairs to the stranger. Mrs. Walsing-

ham had hired her in Brussels, and brought her
home as nurse to the little girl, whose previous nurse
had been dismissed for bad conduct in that city.

'Mrs. Walsingham's little girl?' inquired Sir
Cyprian.

'No. The darling is an orphan, the daughter
of a poor cousin of Mrs. Walsingham, who died
in Vienna, and the kind lady brought the little
one home, and is going to bring her up as her own
child.'

Sir Cyprian heard and was doubtful. He had
his own theory about this baby, but a theory which
he would not for worlds have imparted to any one.
He got on quite familiar terms with the little one
by-and-by. She was a chubby rosy infant of about
fifteen months old, with brown eyes and fair complexion, and hair that made golden-brown rings upon
her ivory forehead. She made frantic efforts to talk,
but at present only succeeded in being loquacious in
a language of her own.

She was quite ready to attach herself to the wandering stranger, fascinated by his watch-chain and
seals.

'What is her name?' asked Sir Cyprian.

'Clara, but we always call her Baby.'

'Clara? That's only her Christian name; she has a surname, I suppose?'

The nursemaid supposed as much also, but had never heard any surname, nor the profession of the little dear's father, nor any details of the death of father and mother. Mrs. Walsingham was a lady who talked very little, but she seemed extremely fond of baby. She came to see her twice a week, and sometimes stayed all day, playing with her, and superintending her dinner, and carrying her about the garden.

On the morning after that interview with James Wyatt, Sir Cyprian rode to Totteridge and put up his horse, as usual, at the little inn. The nurse had told him that Mrs. Walsingham was to be at the cottage to-day, and he had special reasons for wishing to see that lady. He might have called upon her in Half-moon Street, of course, but he preferred to see her at Baby's establishment, if possible.

It was noon when he walked up and down the pathway before the cottage, waiting for Mrs.

Walsingham's arrival, a bright winter day, with a blue sky and a west wind. He had exchanged greetings with Baby already, that young lady saluting him from the nursery window with vivacious flourishes of her pink arms.

The church clock had not long struck twelve when Mrs. Walsingham's neat brougham drove up. She opened the door and let herself out, and had scarcely stepped on to the pathway, when she recognised Sir Cyprian.

She turned very pale, and made a little movement, as if she would have gone back to her carriage, but Sir Cyprian advanced, hat in hand, to greet her.

'You have not forgotten me, I hope, Mrs. Walsingham?'

'Sir Cyprian Davenant, I think?'

'Yes. I had the pleasure of meeting you more than three years ago at the "Star and Garter."'

'I remember perfectly. You have been in Africa since then. I have read some notices of your adventures there. I am glad to see you so little the worse for your travels. And now I must bid you good morning. I have to see some people here. You can wait at the inn, Holmes," to the coachman.

' Will you give me half an hour—a quarter of an hour's conversation, Mrs. Walsingham ? ' asked Sir Cyprian.

She looked at him uneasily, evidently puzzled.

' Upon what subject ? '

' Upon a matter of life and death.'

'You alarm me. Have you come here on purpose to waylay me ? I thought our meeting was accidental ? '

' Waylay is a disagreeable word; but I certainly came here this morning on purpose to see you. I am going to make an appeal to your heart, Mrs. Walsingham. I want you to do a noble action.'

' I am afraid you have come to the wrong quarter for that commodity,' she answered, with a bitter smile; but she seemed somewhat reassured by this mode of address.

' Shall we walk ? ' she asked, moving away from the garden gate.

The wide high road lay before them, destitute

of any sign of human life, the leafless limes and chestnuts standing up against the winter sky, the far-off hills purple in the clear bright air. They would be as much alone here as within any four walls, and Mrs. Walsingham was evidently disinclined to admit Sir Cyprian into Ivy Cottage, as the house with the green shutters was called.

'Have you friends here? Do you often come?' asked Mrs. Walsingham, carelessly.

'I take my morning ride here occasionally, and the other day, while resting my horse, I made the acquaintance of your German nurse and her charge. Baby is a most fascinating little thing, and I take the warmest interest in her.'

'What a pity my small cousin is not old enough to appreciate the honour!' sneered Mrs. Walsingham.

Sir Cyprian ignored the sneer.

'My interest in that sweet little thing has given rise to a strange idea—a wild one, you will say, perhaps, when I have explained myself. But I must begin at the beginning.

I told you that I was going to make an appeal
to your heart. I come here to ask you to lend
your aid in saving the life and reason of one
whom you may have deemed in somewise your
rival. Mrs. Sinclair is dying.'

Mrs. Walsingham was silent.

'You have ·heard as much from some one
else, perhaps?'

'I heard that she was seriously ill.'

'And mentally afflicted?'

'Yes. You do not expect me to be greatly shocked
or grieved, I hope? I never saw the lady, except
in her box at the opera.'

'And being a stranger you cannot pity her.
That is not following the example of the good
Samaritan.'

'If I found her on the roadside I should try to
succour her, I dare say,' answered Mrs. Walsingham;
'but as her distresses do not come in my pathway, and as I have many nearer demands upon
my pity, I can hardly be expected to make
myself miserable on Mrs. Sinclair's account. No
doubt she has plenty of sympathy—a husband who

adores her—and the chivalrous devotion of old admirers, like yourself.'

'Spare her your sneers, Mrs. Walsingham. At no moment of her married life has she been a woman to be envied. In her present condition to refuse her pity would be to be less than human. Constance Sinclair is dying of a broken heart.'

'Very sad,' sighed Mrs. Walsingham.

'That is what you would say if one of your friends related the untimely death of a favourite lapdog. Have you ever thought what that phrase means, Mrs. Walsingham? People use it lightly enough. A broken heart—the slow agony of a grief that kills; —a broken heart—not broken by some sudden blow that shatters joy and life together;—happy those whom sorrow slays with such merciful violence,— but the slow wearing away, the dull, hopeless days, the sleepless nights, the despair that eats into the soul, yet is so slow to kill;—these are the agonies which we sum up lightly, in our conventional phraseology, when we talk about broken hearts.'

'Is it the loss of her baby which Mrs. Sinclair feels so deeply?' asked Mrs. Walsingham, who had

listened thoughtfully to Sir Cyprian's appeal. She
no longer affected a callous indifference to her rival's
grief.

'Yes. That is the grief which is killing her.
She has never been really happy with her husband,
though she has been a good and dutiful wife. The
child brought her happiness. She gave it all her
love. She may have erred, perhaps, in concentrating
her affection upon this baby, but the baby represented her world of love. When that was taken
from her—suddenly, without a moment's warning—
she gave herself up to despair. I have talked to a
faithful servant who was with her in that bitter time,
who knew her measureless love for the child. I
have seen her in her grief, seen her the wreck of the
joyous girl I knew three years ago.'

Mrs. Walsingham was moved. No softening tear
veiled the hard brightness of her eyes, but her lower
lip worked nervously, and her increasing pallor
told of a mind deeply troubled.

'If her husband had by any act of his brought
her to this condition, I should call him something
worse than a murderer,' said Sir Cyprian, 'but,

badly as I think of Gilbert Sinclair, I cannot blame him here. It is destiny that has been cruel—an inscrutable Providence which has chosen to inflict this hopeless misery on the gentlest and most innocent of victims. It is very hard to understand why this should be.'

'Mrs. Sinclair is not the first,' said Mrs. Walsingham, struggling against some strong feeling. 'Other women have lost children they loved—only children—the idols of their hearts.'

'Other women have had kinder husbands, perhaps, to sympathize with and comfort them. Other women have had sources of consolation which Mrs. Sinclair has not.'

'She has her piety—her church—her prayer-book. I should have thought so pure and perfect a woman would find consolation from those. I do not profess to be religious—or to have treasures laid up in heaven—and the loss of what I love most on earth might bring *me* to madness. But Mrs. Sinclair's placid perfection should be above such human weakness.'

'She is human enough and weak enough to

break her heart for the loss of her child,' answered
Sir Cyprian, growing angry. 'But you seem to be
incapable of pity, and I fear I have been mistaken
in appealing to you. Yet I thought that your love
for that child yonder might inspire some feeling of
sympathy with an afflicted mother.'

'My affection for my poor little orphan cousin—
a waif thrown on my hands by misfortune—is not a
very absorbing sentiment,' answered Mrs. Walsingham, with languid scorn.

'So much the better,' cried Sir Cyprian,
eagerly, 'for in that case you will the easier fall in
with my plan for saving Mrs. Sinclair's life and
reason.'

'You have a plan for saving her?'

'Yes, a plan recommended by her physicians, and
to which her husband and father have given their
consent. In a crisis in which nothing but hope
could save her she has been told to hope. It has
been even hinted to her that her child is still
living.'

Mrs. Walsingham started, and looked at him
wonderingly.

'A cruel deception, you think ; but the case was desperate, remember. This false hope has already done something. I have heard this morning that there has been a faint rally—a flicker of returning intelligence. She remembers that she has been told to hope—remembers and looks forward to the realization of the promise that has been made. If we fail her now, despair will again take possession of her—more bitter because of this ray of light. The plan formed by those who love her best is to give her a child to love ; a child whom she will believe at first to be her own, saved from the German river ; but about which, in time to come, when reason and strength have returned, she may be told the truth. She will have given the little one her love by that time, and the adopted child will fill the place of the lost one.'

'A most romantic scheme, assuredly, Sir Cyprian. And pray what part do you expect me to play in this domestic drama ? Why choose me for your confidante ?'

'The little girl you have adopted is about the age of Mrs. Sinclair's baby. You admit that she is not very dear to you—a charge which you have taken upon yourself out of charity. Let Gilbert Sinclair adopt that child. He shall provide handsomely for her future, or, if you prefer trusting me, I will settle a sum of money which you shall approve, in trust for your little cousin, you yourself choosing the trustees. Give me that dear child, Mrs. Walsingham, and you will be the means of saving Constance Sinclair's life.'

'That child?' cried Mrs. Walsingham, looking at him with wide open eyes. 'I give you *that* child —to be Constance Sinclair's solace and consolation —to win Gilbert's wife back to life and happiness? *I* surrender that child! You must be mad to ask it.'

'Did you not tell me just now that the child was not especially dear to you?'

'She is dear to me,' answered Mrs. Walsingham, vehemently. 'I have grown to love her. She is all I have in the world to love. She reminds me of one who once loved me. Why do you prate to me of Mrs. Sinclair's loneliness? She cannot be lonelier than I am. What is there but emptiness in my heart? Yet I do not complain of a broken heart. *I* do not abandon myself to madness or imbecility. I bear my burden. Let her bear hers. Give you that child, indeed! That is asking too much.'

'Pardon me, Mrs. Walsingham. I thought I was talking to a woman with a noble nature, whose higher instincts only needed to be appealed to.'

'It is so long since people have left off appealing to my higher instincts that they have somewhat lost their use. Do you think, Sir Cyprian Davenant, that I have cause to love or pity, or sacrifice myself for Constance Sinclair? You should know better than that, unless you have lived all these years in this world without knowing what kind of clay your fellow-men and women are made of. I have the strongest reason to detest Mrs. Sinclair, and I do detest her, frankly. She has done me no wrong, you will say. She has done me the greatest wrong —robbed me of the man I love, of wealth, status, name, and place in the world. Do you think it matters to me that she was unconscious of that wrong? She has done it, and I hate her for it, and shall so hate her till my dying day.'

'Your hatred will not reach her in her grave or follow her beyond it,' answered Sir Cyprian. 'Your pity might save her life.'

'Find some hospital brat to palm upon this distracted mother—some baby-farmer's *protegée*.'

'I will find some respectably born child, be sure, Mrs. Walsingham. It was only a fancy, perhaps, which led me to propose taking your little kinswoman. I counted too much upon the generosity of a disappointed rival.'

And with this home-thrust Sir Cyprian bowed, and walked away, leaving the lady to her own reflections.

A woman of this kind, a being swayed by passion, is often a mass of inconsistency and contradiction, now hot, now cold. At a late hour that evening Sir Cyprian received a letter, delivered by a man-servant. It was from Mrs. Walsingham.

'I am the most wretched of women,' she wrote, 'utterly weary of life. Mrs. Sinclair may have the child. She would grow up a wretch if she grew up under my influence, for every day makes me more miserable and more bitter. What shall I be as an old woman? Send some trustworthy person to fetch the little girl to-morrow. I give her up to you entirely, but upon condition that Mrs. Sinclair shall never know to whom she owes her adopted child. May the adoption prosper; but as I hear that Mr. Sinclair is in a fair way to ruin, I do not think you are giving my young kinswoman a very brilliant start in life. Be this as it may, I wash my hands of her. She has not brought me happiness; and perhaps if I were to let her wind herself round my heart it might prove by-and-by that I had taught a serpent to coil there. I have not too good an opinion of her blood.—Your's truly,

'CLARA WALSINGHAM.

'Half-moon Street,
  'Wednesday night.'

CHAPTER XXII.

KILL OR CURE.

MR. SINCLAIR was told by Lord Clanyarde of the plan which had been devised by the German physician for his daughter's cure, and after a lengthy discussion gave his sullen consent to the imposture.

'I don't like your German doctor—a thorough-paced charlatan, I'll warrant,' he said, 'and I don't like palming off an impostor upon my poor wife. But if you see any chance of good from this experiment let it be tried. God knows I would give my heart's blood to bring Constance back to health and reason.'

This was said with an unmistakable earnestness, and Lord Clanyarde believed it. He did not know what bitter reason Gilbert Sinclair had for desiring his wife's recovery, in the guilty consciousness that his brutality was the chief cause of her illness.

' You are not going to bring some low-born brat
into my house, I hope ? ' said Gilbert, with the
pride of a man whose grandfather had worked
in the mines, and whose father had died worth a
million.

' No, we shall find a gentleman's child—some
orphan of about Christabel's age—to adopt.'

Gilbert shrugged his shoulders, and said no
more.

That visit of the German physician had certainly
wrought a change in Constance Sinclair's condition,
and Dr. Webb declared that the change was for the
better. She seemed to have awakened from that
dull apathy, that utter inertness of mind and body,
which both the London · physician and the faithful
country watch-dog had taken to be the precursor of
death. She was restless—fluttered by some expectation which kept her senses curiously on the alert—
wistful — watchful — listening — starting at every
opening of a door—at every coming footfall.

On the morning after Dr. Hollendorf's visit, she
asked for her Bible, and began to read David's Psalms
of thanksgiving and rejoicing aloud, like one who

gave thanks for a great joy. Later in the same day she went to the piano and sang—sang as she had never done since the beginning of her illness—sang like one who pours forth the gladness of her heart in melody.

When Dr. Webb came that afternoon, he found his patient sitting in an arm-chair by the window, propped up with pillows, much to the disgust of Melanie Duport, who was on duty at this time.

'I know she isn't strong enough to sit up,' said Melanie to the doctor, 'but she would do it. She seems to be watching for something, or some one.'

The long window opening upon the balcony commanded a distant curve of the drive leading up to the house, and it was on this point that Constance Sinclair's eyes were fixed.

'What are you watching for, dear lady?' asked Dr. Webb, in his bland voice, that caressing tone in which medical men address feminine and infantine patients. In Dr. Webb's case the blandness meant more than it usually does, for he really loved his patient.

'1 am watching for my child. They will bring her to-day, perhaps. The strange doctor told me she was not drowned. It was true, wasn't it? He wouldn't deceive me. There was something in his voice that made me trust him—something that went to my heart. My darling was saved, and she is coming back to me. You won't deceive me, I know. She is coming—soon—soon—soon! Dear, dearest Dr. Webb, is it true?'

'Dear Mrs. Sinclair, you must not agitate yourself in this way,' cried the doctor, flattered by this address. 'Yes, yes, Lord Clanyarde is going to bring you the little girl; and you'll be very fond of her, I hope—and feel quite happy again.'

'Happy?' cried Constance, 'I shall be in heaven! Ask papa to bring her soon.'

She was restless throughout that day—sleepless all night. Sometimes her mind wandered, but at other times she spoke clearly and reasonably of God's goodness to her in saving her child. On the following day the same idea was still paramount, but she was somewhat weakened by her excitement and restlessness, and was no longer able to sit up at her post of obseivation by the window. As the day wore on the old dull apathy seemed to be creeping over her again. She lay on her couch by the fire, silent, exhausted, noticing nothing that occurred around her; her pulse was alarmingly weak, her eyes vacant and heavy.

'If they don't bring the child soon, it will be too late for their experiment,' thought Dr. Webb. 'And if they do bring it, the excitement may be fatal. God guide us aright!'

It was dusk when Lord Clanyarde's brougham drove up to the porch, and his lordship alighted, carrying a child, muffled in soft woollen shawls, and fast asleep. Gilbert Sinclair had not yet returned from his daily ride. The house was dark and empty.

Lord Clanyarde went straight to his daughter's room, where Dr. Webb was sitting, too anxious to leave his patient till the crisis which the intended experiment might produce had passed safely. Dr. Webb was not particularly hopeful about the strange doctor's plan.

'Such good news, my darling!' said Lord Clanyarde, with elaborate cheerfulness. 'Pray don't agitate yourself, my dear Constance.'

She had started up from her sofa already, and tottered towards him with outstretched arms.

'I have brought you your baby. The little pet was not drowned after all, and some good people in Germany took care of her. You will find her changed, of course; three or four months makes such a difference in a baby.'

Constance neither heeded nor heard. She was sitting on the floor with the newly awakened child in her lap, hugging it to her breast, weeping sweetest tears over the soft curly head, breathing forth her rapture in low inarticulate exclamations. The firelight shone on the picture of mother and child clinging together thus—the little one submitting uncomplainingly to those vehement caresses.

'Thank God!' ejaculated Lord Clanyarde within himself. 'She doesn't ask a question, poor child. She hasn't the faintest suspicion that we're deceiving her.'

He had chosen this hour for the introduction of the infant impostor, so that Constance's first scrutiny of the baby features should take place in a doubtful light. If first impressions were but favourable, doubts could hardly arise afterwards in that enfeebled mind. Only when reason was fully restored would Constance begin to ask awkward questions.

In this happy hour she did not even scrutinize the baby face—she only covered it with tears and kisses, and laid it against her bosom, and was content. She accepted this baby stranger at once as her lost Christabel.

Dr. Webb was delighted. Those tears, those caresses, those gushes of happy love! What medicines could work such cure for a mind astray?

'Upon my word, I believe you have done the right thing, and that your German doctor is not such a quack as I thought him,' whispered the little man to Lord Clanyarde.

He had still better reason to say this three or four hours later, when Constance was sleeping tranquilly—a sound and healthy slumber such as she had not known for many weary weeks—with the baby nestling at her side.

Mr. Sinclair heard of the success that had attended the experiment, and seemed glad; or as glad as a man could be who had pressing cause for trouble.

END OF VOL. I.

J. AND W. RIDER, PRINTERS, LONDON.